# A Family Man by John Galsworthy

John Galsworthy first published in 1897 with a collection of short stories entitled "The Four Winds". For the next 7 years he published these and all works under his pen name John Sinjohn. It was only upon the death of his father and the publication of "The Island Pharisees" in 1904 that he published as John Galsworthy. His first play was The Silver Box, an immediate success when it debuted in 1906 and was followed by "The Man of Property" later that same year and was the first in the Forsyte trilogy. Whilst today he is far more well know as a Nobel Prize winning novelist then he was considered a playwright dealing with social issues and the class system. We publish here 'A Family Man' a great example of both his writing and his demonstration of how the class system worked at the time. He was appointed to the Order of Merit in 1929, after earlier turning down a knighthood, and awarded the Nobel Prize in 1932 though he was too ill to attend. John Galsworthy died from a brain tumour at his London home, Grove Lodge, Hampstead on January 31st 1933. In accordance with his will he was cremated at Woking with his ashes then being scattered over the South Downs from an aeroplane.

## Index Of Contents

## CHARACTERS

JOHN BUILDER............of the firm of Builder & Builder
JULIA....................... ...His Wife
ATHENE.....................His elder Daughter
MAUD...................... His younger Daughter
RALPH BUILDER..........His Brother, and Partner
GUY HERRINGHAME...A Flying Man
ANNIE..................... A Young Person in Blue
CAMILLE.................... Mrs Builder's French Maid
TOPPING....................Builder's Manservant
THE MAYOR...............Of Breconridge
HARRIS...................... His Secretary
FRANCIS CHANTREY... J.P.
MOON.......................A Constable
MARTIN.....................A Police Sergeant
A JOURNALIST...........From The Comet
THE FIGURE OF A POACHER
THE VOICES AND FACES OF SMALL BOYS

The action passes in the town of Breconridge, the Midlands.

⌐R'S Study. After breakfast.

⌐chtime.

SCENE I. THE MAYOR'S Study. 10am the following day.
SCENE II. BUILDER'S Study. The same. Noon.
SCENE III. BUILDER'S Study. The same. Evening.

## ACT I

### SCENE I

The study of JOHN BUILDER in the provincial town of Breconridge. A panelled room wherein nothing is ever studied, except perhaps BUILDER'S face in the mirror over the fireplace. It is, however, comfortable, and has large leather chairs and a writing table in the centre, on which is a typewriter, and many papers. At the back is a large window with French outside shutters, overlooking the street, for the house is an old one, built in an age when the homes of doctors, lawyers and so forth were part of a provincial town, and not yet suburban. There are two or three fine old prints on the walls, Right and Left; and a fine, old fireplace, Left, with a fender on which one can sit. A door, Left back, leads into the dining-room, and a door, Right forward, into the hall. JOHN BUILDER is sitting in his after-breakfast chair before the fire with The Times in his hands. He has breakfasted well, and is in that condition of first-pipe serenity in which the affairs of the nation seem almost bearable. He is a tallish, square, personable man of forty-seven, with a well-coloured, jowly, fullish face, marked under the eyes, which have very small pupils and a good deal of light in them. His bearing has force and importance, as of a man accustomed to rising and ownerships, sure in his opinions, and not lacking in geniality when things go his way. Essentially a Midlander. His wife, a woman of forty-one, of ivory tint, with a thin, trim figure and a face so strangely composed as to be almost like a mask (essentially from Jersey) is putting a nib into a pen-holder, and filling an inkpot at the writing-table. As the curtain rises CAMILLE enters with a rather broken-down cardboard box containing flowers. She is a young woman with a good figure, a pale face, the warm brown eyes and complete poise of a Frenchwoman. She takes the box to MRS BUILDER. MRS BUILDER. The blue vase, please, Camille. CAMILLE fetches a vase. MRS BUILDER puts the flowers into the vase. CAMILLE gathers up the debris; and with a glance at BUILDER goes out.

BUILDER. Glorious October! I ought to have a damned good day's shooting with Chantrey tomorrow.

MRS BUILDER. [Arranging the flowers] Aren't you going to the office this morning?

BUILDER. Well, no, I was going to take a couple of days off. If you feel at the top of your form, take a rest—then you go on feeling at the top. [He looks at her, as if calculating] What do you say to looking up Athene?

MRS BUILDER. [Palpably astonished] Athene? But you said you'd done with her?

BUILDER. [Smiling] Six weeks ago; but, dash it, one can't have done with one's own daughter. That's the weakness of an Englishman; he can't keep up his resentments. In a town like this it doesn't do to have her living by herself. One of these days it'll get out we've had a row. That wouldn't do me any good.

MRS BUILDER. I see.

BUILDER. Besides, I miss her. Maud's so self-absorbed. It makes a big hole in the family, Julia. You'v' got her address, haven't you?

MRS BUILDER. Yes. [Very still] But do you think it's dignified, John?

BUILDER. [Genially] Oh, hang dignity! I rather pride myself on knowing when to stand on my dignity and when to sit on it. If she's still crazy about Art, she can live at home, and go out to study.

MRS BUILDER. Her craze was for liberty.

BUILDER. A few weeks' discomfort soon cures that. She can't live on her pittance. She'll have found that out by now. Get your things on and come with me at twelve o'clock.

MRS BUILDER. I think you'll regret it. She'll refuse.

BUILDER. Not if I'm nice to her. A child could play with me to-day. Shall I tell you a secret, Julia?

MRS BUILDER. It would be pleasant for a change.

BUILDER. The Mayor's coming round at eleven, and I know perfectly well what he's coming for.

MRS BUILDER. Well?

BUILDER. I'm to be nominated for Mayor next month. Harris tipped me the wink at the last Council meeting. Not so bad at forty-seven—h'm? I can make a thundering good Mayor. I can do things for this town that nobody else can.

MRS BUILDER. Now I understand about Athene.

BUILDER. [Good-humouredly] Well, it's partly that. But [more seriously] it's more the feeling I get that I'm not doing my duty by her. Goodness knows whom she may be picking up with! Artists are a loose lot. And young people in these days are the limit. I quite believe in moving with the times, but one's either born a Conservative, or one isn't. So you be ready at twelve, see. By the way, that French maid of yours, Julia—

MRS BUILDER. What about her?

BUILDER. Is she, er, is she all right? We don't want any trouble with Topping.

MRS BUILDER. There will be none with—Topping. [She opens the door Left.]

BUILDER. I don't know; she strikes me as very French.

MRS BUILDER smiles and passes out. BUILDER fills his second pipe. He is just taking up the paper again when the door from the hall is opened, and the manservant TOPPING, dried, dark, sub-humorous, in a black cut-away, announces:

TOPPING. The Mayor, Sir, and Mr Harris!

THE MAYOR of Breconridge enters, He is clean-shaven, red-faced, light-eyed, about sixty, shrewd, poll-parroty, naturally jovial, dressed with the indefinable wrongness of a burgher; he is followed by his Secretary HARRIS, a man all eyes and cleverness. TOPPING retires.

BUILDER. [Rising] Hallo, Mayor! What brings you so early? Glad to see you. Morning, Harris!

MAYOR. Morning, Builder, morning.

HARRIS. Good-morning, Sir.

BUILDER. Sit down-sit down! Have a cigar!

The MAYOR takes a cigar HARRIS a cigarette from his own case.

BUILDER. Well, Mayor, what's gone wrong with the works?

He and HARRIS exchange a look.

MAYOR. [With his first puff] After you left the Council the other day, Builder, we came to a decision.

BUILDER. Deuce you did! Shall I agree with it?

MAYOR. We shall see. We want to nominate you for Mayor. You willin' to stand?

BUILDER. [Stolid] That requires consideration.

MAYOR. The only alternative is Chantrey; but he's a light weight, and rather too much County. What's your objection?

BUILDER. It's a bit unexpected, Mayor. [Looks at HARRIS] Am I the right man? Following you, you know. I'm shooting with Chantrey to-morrow. What does he feel about it?

MAYOR. What do you say, 'Arris?

HARRIS. Mr Chantrey's a public school and University man, Sir; he's not what I call ambitious.

BUILDER. Nor am I, Harris.

HARRIS. No, sir; of course you've a high sense of duty. Mr Chantrey's rather dilettante.

MAYOR. We want a solid man.

BUILDER. I'm very busy, you know, Mayor.

MAYOR. But you've got all the qualifications—big business, family man, live in the town, church-goer, experience on the Council and the Bench. Better say "yes," Builder.

BUILDER. It's a lot of extra work. I don't take things up lightly.

MAYOR. Dangerous times, these. Authority questioned all over the place. We want a man that feels his responsibilities, and we think we've got him in you.

BUILDER. Very good of you, Mayor. I don't know, I'm sure. I must think of the good of the town.

HARRIS. I shouldn't worry about that, sir.

MAYOR. The name John Builder carries weight. You're looked up to as a man who can manage his own affairs. Madam and the young ladies well?

BUILDER. First-rate.

MAYOR. [Rises] That's right. Well, if you'd like to talk it over with Chantrey to-morrow. With all this extremism, we want a man of principle and common sense.

HARRIS. We want a man that'll grasp the nettle, sir—and that's you.

BUILDER. Hm! I've got a temper, you know.

MAYOR. [Chuckling] We do—we do! You'll say "yes," I see. No false modesty! Come along, 'Arris, we must go.

BUILDER. Well, Mayor, I'll think it over, and let you have an answer. You know my faults, and you know my qualities, such as they are. I'm just a plain Englishman.

MAYOR. We don't want anything better than that. I always say the great point about an Englishman is that he's got bottom; you may knock him off his pins, but you find him on 'em again before you can say "Jack Robinson." He may have his moments of aberration, but he's a sticker. Morning, Builder, morning! Hope you'll say "yes."

He shakes hands and goes out, followed by HARRIS. When the door is dosed BUILDER stands a moment quite still with a gratified smile on his face; then turns and scrutinises himself in the glass over the hearth. While he is doing so the door from the dining-room is opened quietly and CAMILLE comes in. BUILDER, suddenly seeing her reflected in the mirror, turns.

BUILDER. What is it, Camille?

CAMILLE. Madame send me for a letter she say you have, Monsieur, from the dyer and cleaner, with a bill.

BUILDER. [Feeling in his pockets] Yes—no. It's on the table.

CAMILLE goes to the writing-table and looks. That blue thing.

CAMILLE. [Taking it up] Non, Monsieur, this is from the gas.

BUILDER. Oh! Ah! [He moves up to the table and turns over papers. CAMILLE stands motionless close by with her eyes fixed on him.] Here it is! [He looks up, sees her looking at him, drops his own gaze, and hands her the letter. Their hands touch. Putting his hands in his pockets] What made you come to England?

CAMILLE. [Demure] It is better pay, Monsieur, and [With a smile] the English are so amiable.

BUILDER. Deuce they are! They haven't got that reputation.

CAMILLE. Oh! I admire Englishmen. They are so strong and kind.

BUILDER. [Bluffly flattered] H'm! We've no manners.

CAMILLE. The Frenchman is more polite, but not in the 'eart.

BUILDER. Yes. I suppose we're pretty sound at heart.

CAMILLE. And the Englishman have his life in the family—the Frenchman have his life outside.

BUILDER. [With discomfort] H'm!

CAMILLE. [With a look] Too mooch in the family—like a rabbit in a 'utch.

BUILDER. Oh! So that's your view of us! [His eyes rest on her, attracted but resentful].

CAMILLE. Pardon, Monsieur, my tongue run away with me.

BUILDER. [Half conscious of being led on] Are you from Paris?

CAMILLE. [Clasping her hands] Yes. What a town for pleasure—Paris!

BUILDER. I suppose so. Loose place, Paris.

CAMILLE. Loose? What is that, Monsieur?

BUILDER. The opposite of strict.

CAMILLE. Strict! Oh! certainly we like life, we other French. It is not like England. I take this to Madame, Monsieur. [She turns as if to go] Excuse me.

BUILDER. I thought you Frenchwomen all married young.

CAMILLE. I 'ave been married; my 'usband did die—en Afrique.

BUILDER. You wear no ring.

CAMILLE. [Smiling] I prefare to be mademoiselle, Monsieur.

BUILDER. [Dubiously] Well, it's all the same to us. [He takes a letter up from the table] You might take this to Mrs Builder too. [Again their fingers touch, and there is a suspicion of encounter between their eyes.]

CAMILLE goes out.

BUILDER. [Turning to his chair] Don't know about that woman—she's a tantalizer.

He compresses his lips, and is settling back into his chair, when the door from the hall is opened and his daughter MAUD comes in; a pretty girl, rather pale, with fine eyes. Though her face has a determined cast her manner at this moment is by no means decisive. She has a letter in her hand, and advances rather as if she were stalking her father, who, after a "Hallo, Maud!" has begun to read his paper.

MAUD. [Getting as far as the table] Father.

BUILDER. [Not lowering the paper] Well? I know that tone. What do you want—money?

MAUD. I always want money, of course; but—but—

BUILDER. [Pulling out a note-abstractedly] Here's five pounds for you.

MAUD, advancing, takes it, then seems to find what she has come for more on her chest than ever.

BUILDER. [Unconscious] Will you take a letter for me?

MAUD sits down Left of table and prepares to take down the letter.

[Dictating] "Dear Mr Mayor, Referring to your call this morning, I have, er, given the matter very careful consideration, and though somewhat reluctant—"

MAUD. Are you really reluctant, father?

BUILDER. Go on—"To assume greater responsibilities, I feel it my duty to come forward in accordance with your wish. The—er—honour is one of which I hardly feel myself worthy, but you may rest assured—"

MAUD. Worthy. But you do, you know.

BUILDER. Look here! Are you trying to get a rise out of me?—because you won't succeed this morning.

MAUD. I thought you were trying to get one out of me.

BUILDER. Well, how would you express it?

MAUD. "I know I'm the best man for the place, and so do you—"

BUILDER. The disrespect of you young people is something extraordinary. And that reminds me where do you go every evening now after tea?

MAUD. I, I don't know.

BUILDER. Come now, that won't do—you're never in the house from six to seven.

MAUD. Well! It has to do with my education.

BUILDER. Why, you finished that two years ago!

MAUD. Well, call it a hobby, if you like, then, father.

She takes up the letter she brought in and seems on the point of broaching it.

BUILDER. Hobby? Well, what is it?

MAUD. I don't want to irritate you, father.

BUILDER. You can't irritate me more than by having secrets. See what that led to in your sister's case. And, by the way, I'm going to put an end to that this morning. You'll be glad to have her back, won't you?

MAUD. [Startled] What!

BUILDER. Your mother and I are going round to Athene at twelve o'clock. I shall make it up with her. She must come back here.

MAUD. [Aghast, but hiding it] Oh! It's, it's no good, father. She won't.

BUILDER. We shall see that. I've quite got over my tantrum, and I expect she has.

MAUD. [Earnestly] Father! I do really assure you she won't; it's only wasting your time, and making you eat humble pie.

BUILDER. Well, I can eat a good deal this morning. It's all nonsense! A family's a family.

MAUD. [More and more disturbed, but hiding it] Father, if I were you, I wouldn't-really! It's not-dignified.

BUILDER. You can leave me to judge of that. It's not dignified for the Mayor of this town to have an unmarried daughter as young as Athene living by herself away from home. This idea that she's on a visit won't wash any longer. Now finish that letter—"worthy, but you may rest assured that I shall do my best to sustain the—er—dignity of the office." [MAUD types desperately.] Got that? "And—er—preserve the tradition so worthily—" No— "so staunchly"—er—er—

MAUD. Upheld.

BUILDER. Ah! "—upheld by yourself. Faithfully yours."

MAUD. [Finishing] Father, you thought Athene went off in a huff. It wasn't that a bit. She always meant to go. She just got you into a rage to make it easier. She hated living at home.

BUILDER. Nonsense! Why on earth should she?

MAUD. Well, she did! And so do— [Checking herself] And so you see it'll only make you ridiculous to go.

BUILDER. [Rises] Now what's behind this, Maud?

MAUD. Behind—Oh! nothing!

BUILDER. The fact is, you girls have been spoiled, and you enjoy twisting my tail; but you can't make me roar this morning. I'm too pleased with things. You'll see, it'll be all right with Athene.

MAUD. [Very suddenly] Father!

BUILDER. [Grimly humorous] Well! Get it off your chest. What's that letter about?

MAUD. [Failing again and crumpling the letter behind her back] Oh! nothing.

BUILDER. Everything's nothing this morning. Do you know what sort of people Athene associates with now—I suppose you see her?

MAUD. Sometimes.

BUILDER. Well?

MAUD. Nobody much. There isn't anybody here to associate with. It's all hopelessly behind the times.

BUILDER. Oh! you think so! That's the inflammatory fiction you pick up. I tell you what, young woman—the sooner you and your sister get rid of your silly notions about not living at home, and making your own way, the sooner you'll both get married and make it. Men don't like the new spirit in women—they may say they do, but they don't.

MAUD. You don't, father, I know.

BUILDER. Well, I'm very ordinary. If you keep your eyes open, you'll soon see that.

MAUD. Men don't like freedom for anybody but themselves.

BUILDER. That's not the way to put it. [Tapping out his pipe] Women in your class have never had to face realities.

MAUD. No, but we want to.

BUILDER. [Good-humouredly] Well, I'll bet you what you like, Athene's dose of reality will have cured her.

MAUD. And I'll bet you—No, I won't!

BUILDER. You'd better not. Athene will come home, and only too glad to do it. Ring for Topping and order the car at twelve.

As he opens the door to pass out, MAUD starts forward, but checks herself.

MAUD. [Looking at her watch] Half-past eleven! Good heavens!

She goes to the bell and rings. Then goes back to the table, and writes an address on a bit of paper. TOPPING enters Right.

TOPPING. Did you ring, Miss?

MAUD. [With the paper] Yes. Look here, Topping! Can you manage— on your bicycle—now at once? I want to send a message to Miss Athene—awfully important. It's just this: "Look out! Father is coming." [Holding out the paper] Here's her address. You must get there and away again by twelve. Father and mother want the car then to go there. Order it before you go. It won't take you twenty minutes on your bicycle. It's down by the river near the ferry. But you mustn't be seen by them either going or coming.

TOPPING. If I should fall into their hands, Miss, shall I eat the despatch?

MAUD. Rather! You're a brick, Topping. Hurry up!

TOPPING. Nothing more precise, Miss?

MAUD. M—m—No.

TOPPING. Very good, Miss Maud. [Conning the address] "Briary Studio, River Road. Look out! Father is coming!" I'll go out the back way. Any answer?

MAUD. No.

TOPPING nods his head and goes out.

MAUD. [To herself] Well, it's all I can do.

She stands, considering, as the CURTAIN falls.


**SCENE II**

The Studio, to which are attached living rooms, might be rented at eighty pounds a year—some painting and gear indeed, but an air of life rather than of work. Things strewn about. Bare walls, a sloping skylight, no windows; no fireplace visible; a bedroom door, stage Right; a kitchen door, stage Left. A door, Centre back, into the street. The door knocker is going.

From the kitchen door, Left, comes the very young person, ANNIE, in blotting-paper blue linen, with a white Dutch cap. She is pretty, her cheeks rosy, and her forehead puckered. She opens the street door. Standing outside is TOPPING. He steps in a pace or two.

TOPPING. Miss Builder live here?

ANNIE. Oh! no, sir; Mrs Herringhame.

TOPPING. Mrs Herringhame? Oh! young lady with dark hair and large expressive eyes?

ANNIE. Oh! yes, sir.

TOPPING. With an "A. B." on her linen? [Moves to table].

ANNIE. Yes, sir.

TOPPING. And "Athene Builder" on her drawings?

ANNIE. [Looking at one] Yes, sir.

TOPPING. Let's see. [He examines the drawing] Mrs Herringhame, you said?

ANNIE. Oh! yes, Sir.

TOPPING. Wot oh!

ANNIE. Did you want anything, sir?

TOPPING. Drop the "sir," my dear; I'm the Builders' man. Mr Herringhame in?

ANNIE. Oh! no, Sir.

TOPPING. Take a message. I can't wait. From Miss Maud Builder. "Look out! Father is coming." Now, whichever of 'em comes in first—that's the message, and don't you forget it.

ANNIE. Oh! no, Sir.

TOPPING. So they're married?

ANNIE. Oh! I don't know, sir.

TOPPING. I see. Well, it ain't known to Builder, J.P., either. That's why there's a message. See?

ANNIE. Oh! yes, Sir.

TOPPING. Keep your head. I must hop it. From Miss Maud Builder. "Look out! Father is coming."

He nods, turns and goes, pulling the door to behind him. ANNIE stands "baff" for a moment.

ANNIE. Ah!

She goes across to the bedroom on the Right, and soon returns with a suit of pyjamas, a toothbrush, a pair of slippers and a case of razors, which she puts on the table, and disappears into the kitchen. She reappears with a bread pan, which she deposits in the centre of the room; then crosses again to the bedroom, and once more reappears with a clothes brush, two hair brushes, and a Norfolk jacket. As she stuffs all these into the bread pan and bears it back into the kitchen, there is the sound of a car driving up and stopping. ANNIE reappears at the kitchen door just as the knocker sounds.

ANNIE. Vexin' and provokin'! [Knocker again. She opens the door] Oh!

MR and MRS BUILDER enter.

BUILDER. Mr and Mrs Builder. My daughter in?

ANNIE. [Confounded] Oh! Sir, no, sir.

BUILDER. My good girl, not "Oh! Sir, no, sir." Simply: No, Sir. See?

ANNIE. Oh! Sir, yes, Sir.

BUILDER. Where is she?

ANNIE. Oh! Sir, I don't know, Sir.

BUILDER. [Fixing her as though he suspected her of banter] Will she be back soon?

ANNIE. No, Sir.

BUILDER. How do you know?

ANNIE. I d—don't, sir.

BUILDER. They why do you say so? [About to mutter "She's an idiot!" he looks at her blushing face and panting figure, pats her on the shoulder and says] Never mind; don't be nervous.

ANNIE. Oh! yes, sir. Is that all, please, sir?

MRS BUILDER. [With a side look at her husband and a faint smile] Yes; you can go.

ANNIE. Thank you, ma'am.

She turns and hurries out into the kitchen, Left. BUILDER gazes after her, and MRS BUILDER gazes at BUILDER with her faint smile.

BUILDER. [After the girl is gone] Quaint and Dutch—pretty little figure! [Staring round] H'm! Extraordinary girls are! Fancy Athene preferring this to home. What?

MRS BUILDER. I didn't say anything.

BUILDER. [Placing a chair for his wife, and sitting down himself] Well, we must wait, I suppose. Confound that Nixon legacy! If Athene hadn't had that potty little legacy left her, she couldn't have done this. Well, I daresay it's all spent by now. I made a mistake to lose my temper with her.

MRS BUILDER. Isn't it always a mistake to lose one's temper?

BUILDER. That's very nice and placid; sort of thing you women who live sheltered lives can say. I often wonder if you women realise the strain on a business man.

MRS BUILDER. [In her softly ironical voice] It seems a shame to add the strain of family life.

BUILDER. You've always been so passive. When I want a thing, I've got to have it.

MRS BUILDER. I've noticed that.

BUILDER. [With a short laugh] Odd if you hadn't, in twenty-three years. [Touching a canvas standing against the chair with his toe] Art! Just a pretext. We shall be having Maud wanting to cut loose next. She's very restive. Still, I oughtn't to have had that scene with Athene. I ought to have put quiet pressure.

MRS BUILDER Smiles.

BUILDER. What are you smiling at?

MRS BUILDER shrugs her shoulders.

Look at this—Cigarettes! [He examines the brand on the box] Strong, very—and not good! [He opens the door] Kitchen! [He shuts it, crosses, and opens the door, Right] Bedroom!

MRS BUILDER. [To his disappearing form] Do you think you ought, John?

He has disappeared, and she ends with an expressive movement of her hands, a long sigh, and a closing of her eyes. BUILDER'S peremptory voice is heard: "Julia!"

What now?

She follows into the bedroom. The maid ANNIE puts her head out of the kitchen door; she comes out a step as if to fly; then, at BUILDER'S voice, shrinks back into the kitchen.

BUILDER, reappearing with a razor strop in one hand and a shaving-brush in the other, is followed by MRS BUILDER.

BUILDER. Explain these! My God! Where's that girl?

MRS BUILDER. John! Don't! [Getting between him and the kitchen door] It's not dignified.

BUILDER. I don't care a damn.

MRS BUILDER. John, you mustn't. Athene has the tiny beginning of a moustache, you know.

BUILDER. What! I shall stay and clear this up if I have to wait a week. Men who let their daughters—! This age is the limit. [He makes a vicious movement with the strop, as though laying it across someone's back.]

MRS BUILDER. She would never stand that. Even wives object, nowadays.

BUILDER. [Grimly] The war's upset everything. Women are utterly out of hand. Why the deuce doesn't she come?

MRS BUILDER. Suppose you leave me here to see her.

BUILDER. [Ominously] This is my job.

MRS BUILDER. I think it's more mine.

BUILDER. Don't stand there opposing everything I say! I'll go and have another look—[He is going towards the bedroom when the sound of a latchkey in the outer door arrests him. He puts the strop and brush behind his back, and adds in a low voice] Here she is!

MRS BUILDER has approached him, and they have both turned towards the opening door. GUY HERRINGHAME comes in. They are a little out of his line of sight, and he has shut the door before he sees them. When he does, his mouth falls open, and his hand on to the knob of the door. He is a comely young man in Harris tweeds. Moreover, he is smoking. He would speak if he could, but his surprise is too excessive. BUILDER. Well, sir?

GUY. [Recovering a little] I was about to say the same to you, sir.

BUILDER. [Very red from repression] These rooms are not yours, are they?

GUY. Nor yours, sir?

BUILDER. May I ask if you know whose they are?

GUY. My sister's.

BUILDER. Your—you—!

MRS BUILDER. John!

BUILDER. Will you kindly tell me why your sister signs her drawings by the name of my daughter, Athene Builder—and has a photograph of my wife hanging there?

The YOUNG MAN looks at MRS BUILDER and winces, but recovers himself.

GUY. [Boldly] As a matter of fact this is my sister's studio; she's in France—and has a friend staying here.

BUILDER. Oh! And you have a key?

GUY. My sister's.

BUILDER. Does your sister shave?

GUY. I—I don't think so.

BUILDER. No. Then perhaps you'll tell me what these mean? [He takes out the strop and shaving stick].

GUY. Oh! Ah! Those things?

BUILDER. Yes. Now then?

GUY. [Addressing MRS BUILDER] Need we go into this in your presence, ma'am? It seems rather delicate.

BUILDER. What explanation have you got?

GUY. Well, you see—

BUILDER. No lies; out with it!

GUY. [With decision] I prefer to say nothing.

BUILDER. What's your name?

GUY. Guy Herringhame.

BUILDER. Do you live here?

Guy makes no sign.

MRS BUILDER. [To Guy] I think you had better go.

BUILDER. Julia, will you leave me to manage this?

MRS BUILDER. [To Guy] When do you expect my daughter in?

GUY. Now—directly.

MRS BUILDER. [Quietly] Are you married to her?

GUY. Yes. That is—no—o; not altogether, I mean.

BUILDER. What's that? Say that again!

GUY. [Folding his arms] I'm not going to say another word.

BUILDER. I am.

MRS BUILDER. John—please!

BUILDER. Don't put your oar in! I've had wonderful patience so far. [He puts his boot through a drawing] Art! This is what comes of it! Are you an artist?

GUY. No; a flying man. The truth is—

BUILDER. I don't want to hear you speak the truth. I'll wait for my daughter.

GUY. If you do, I hope you'll be so very good as to be gentle. If you get angry I might too, and that would be awfully ugly.

BUILDER. Well, I'm damned!

GUY. I quite understand that, sir. But, as a man of the world, I hope you'll take a pull before she comes, if you mean to stay.

BUILDER. If we mean to stay! That's good!

GUY. Will you have a cigarette?

BUILDER. I—I can't express—

GUY. [Soothingly] Don't try, sir. [He jerks up his chin, listening] I think that's her. [Goes to the door] Yes. Now, please! [He opens the door] Your father and mother, Athene.

ATHENE enters. She is flushed and graceful. Twenty-two, with a short upper lip, a straight nose, dark hair, and glowing eyes. She wears bright colours, and has a slow, musical voice, with a slight lisp.

ATHENE. Oh! How are you, mother dear? This is rather a surprise. Father always keeps his word, so I certainly didn't expect him. [She looks steadfastly at BUILDER, but does not approach].

BUILDER. [Controlling himself with an effort] Now, Athene, what's this?

ATHENE. What's what?

BUILDER. [The strop held out] Are you married to this—this—?

ATHENE. [Quietly] To all intents and purposes.

BUILDER. In law?

ATHENE. No.

BUILDER. My God! You—you—!

ATHENE. Father, don't call names, please.

BUILDER. Why aren't you married to him?

ATHENE. Do you want a lot of reasons, or the real one?

BUILDER. This is maddening! [Goes up stage].

ATHENE. Mother dear, will you go into the other room with Guy? [She points to the door Right].

BUILDER. Why?

ATHENE. Because I would rather she didn't hear the reason.

GUY. [To ATHENE, sotto voce] He's not safe.

ATHENE. Oh! yes; go on.

Guy follows MRS BUILDER, and after hesitation at the door they go out into the bedroom.

BUILDER. Now then!

ATHENE. Well, father, if you want to know the real reason, it's—you.

BUILDER. What on earth do you mean?

ATHENE. Guy wants to marry me. In fact, we—But I had such a stunner of marriage from watching you at home, that I—

BUILDER. Don't be impudent! My patience is at breaking-point, I warn you.

ATHENE. I'm perfectly serious, Father. I tell you, we meant to marry, but so far I haven't been able to bring myself to it. You never noticed how we children have watched you.

BUILDER. Me?

ATHENE. Yes. You and mother, and other things; all sorts of things—

BUILDER. [Taking out a handkerchief and wiping his brow] I really think you're mad.

ATHENE. I'm sure you must, dear.

BUILDER. Don't "dear" me! What have you noticed? D'you mean I'm not a good husband and father?

ATHENE. Look at mother. I suppose you can't, now; you're too used to her.

BUILDER. Of course I'm used to her. What else is marrying for?

ATHENE. That; and the production of such as me. And it isn't good enough, father. You shouldn't have set us such a perfect example.

BUILDER. You're talking the most arrant nonsense I ever heard. [He lifts his hands] I've a good mind to shake it out of you.

ATHENE. Shall I call Guy?

He drops his hands.

Confess that being a good husband and father has tried you terribly. It has us, you know.

BUILDER. [Taking refuge in sarcasm] When you've quite done being funny, perhaps you'll tell me why you've behaved like a common street flapper.

ATHENE. [Simply] I couldn't bear to think of Guy as a family man. That's all—absolutely. It's not his fault; he's been awfully anxious to be one.

BUILDER. You've disgraced us, then; that's what it comes to.

ATHENE. I don't want to be unkind, but you've brought it on yourself.

BUILDER. [Genuinely distracted] I can't even get a glimmer of what you mean. I've never been anything but firm. Impatient, perhaps. I'm not an angel; no ordinary healthy man is. I've never grudged you girls any comfort, or pleasure.

ATHENE. Except wills of our own.

BUILDER. What do you want with wills of your own till you're married?

ATHENE. You forget mother!

BUILDER. What about her?

ATHENE. She's very married. Has she a will of her own?

BUILDER. [Sullenly] She's learnt to know when I'm in the right.

ATHENE. I don't ever mean to learn to know when Guy's in the right. Mother's forty-one, and twenty-three years of that she's been your wife. It's a long time, father. Don't you ever look at her face?

BUILDER. [Troubled in a remote way] Rubbish!

ATHENE. I didn't want my face to get like that.

BUILDER. With such views about marriage, what business had you to go near a man? Come, now!

ATHENE. Because I fell in love.

BUILDER. Love leads to marriage—and to nothing else, but the streets. What an example to your sister!

ATHENE. You don't know Maud any more than you knew me. She's got a will of her own too, I can tell you.

BUILDER. Now, look here, Athene. It's always been my way to face accomplished facts. What's done can't be undone; but it can be remedied. You must marry this young—at once, before it gets out. He's behaved like a ruffian: but, by your own confession, you've behaved worse. You've been bitten by this modern disease, this—this, utter lack of common decency. There's an eternal order in certain things, and marriage is one of them; in fact, it's the chief. Come, now. Give me a promise, and I'll try my utmost to forget the whole thing.

ATHENE. When we quarrelled, father, you said you didn't care what became of me.

BUILDER. I was angry.

ATHENE. So you are now.

BUILDER. Come, Athene, don't be childish! Promise me!

ATHENE. [With a little shudder] No! We were on the edge of it. But now I've seen you again—Poor mother!

BUILDER. [Very angry] This is simply blasphemous. What do you mean by harping on your mother? If you think that—that—she doesn't—that she isn't—

ATHENE. Now, father!

BUILDER. I'm damned if I'll sit down under this injustice. Your mother is—is pretty irritating, I can tell you. She—she—Everything suppressed. And—and no—blood in her!

ATHENE. I knew it!

BUILDER. [Aware that he has confirmed some thought in her that he had no intention of confirming] What's that?

ATHENE. Don't you ever look at your own face, father? When you shave, for instance.

BUILDER. Of course I do.

ATHENE. It isn't satisfied, is it?

BUILDER. I don't know what on earth you mean.

ATHENE. You can't help it, but you'd be ever so much happier if you were a Mohammedan, and two or three, instead of one, had—had learned to know when you were in the right.

BUILDER. 'Pon my soul! This is outrageous!

ATHENE. Truth often is.

BUILDER. Will you be quiet?

ATHENE. I don't ever want to feel sorry for Guy in that way.

BUILDER. I think you're the most immodest—I'm ashamed that you're my daughter. If your another had ever carried on as you are now—

ATHENE. Would you have been firm with her?

BUILDER. [Really sick at heart at this unwonted mockery which meets him at every turn] Be quiet, you—!

ATHENE. Has mother never turned?

BUILDER. You're an unnatural girl! Go your own way to hell!

ATHENE. I am not coming back home, father.

BUILDER. [Wrenching open the door, Right] Julia! Come! We can't stay here.

MRS BUILDER comes forth, followed by GUY.

As for you, sir, if you start by allowing a woman to impose her crazy ideas about marriage on you, all I can say is—I despise you. [He crosses to the outer door, followed by his wife. To ATHENE] I've done with you!

He goes out. MRS BUILDER, who has so far seemed to accompany him, shuts the door quickly and remains in the studio. She stands there with that faint smile on her face, looking at the two young people.

ATHENE. Awfully sorry, mother; but don't you see what a stunner father's given me?

MRS BUILDER. My dear, all men are not alike.

GUY. I've always told her that, ma'am.

ATHENE. [Softly] Oh! mother, I'm so sorry for you.

The handle of the door is rattled, a fist is beaten on it.

[She stamps, and covers her ears] Disgusting!

GUY. Shall I—?

MRS BUILDER. [Shaking her head] I'm going in a moment. [To ATHENE] You owe it to me, Athene.

ATHENE. Oh! if somebody would give him a lesson!

BUILDER's voice: "Julia!"

Have you ever tried, mother?

MRS BUILDER looks at the YOUNG MAN, who turns away out of hearing.

MRS BUILDER. Athene, you're mistaken. I've always stood up to him in my own way.

ATHENE. Oh! but, mother—listen!

The beating and rattling have recommenced, and the voice: "Are you coming?"

[Passionately] And that's family life! Father was all right before he married, I expect. And now it's like this. How you survive—!

MRS BUILDER. He's only in a passion, my dear.

ATHENE. It's wicked.

MRS BUILDER. It doesn't work otherwise, Athene.

A single loud bang on the door.

ATHENE. If he beats on that door again, I shall scream.

MRS BUILDER smiles, shakes her head, and turns to the door.

MRS BUILDER. Now, my dear, you're going to be sensible, to please me. It's really best. If I say so, it must be. It's all comedy, Athene.

ATHENE. Tragedy!

GUY. [Turning to them] Look here! Shall I shift him?

MRS BUILDER shakes her head and opens the door. BUILDER stands there, a furious figure.

BUILDER. Will you come, and leave that baggage and her cad?

MRS BUILDER steps quickly out and the door is closed. Guy makes an angry movement towards it.

ATHENE. Guy!

GUY. [Turning to her] That puts the top hat on. So persuasive! [He takes out of his pocket a wedding ring, and a marriage licence] Well! What's to be done with these pretty things, now?

ATHENE. Burn them!

GUY. [Slowly] Not quite. You can't imagine I should ever be like that, Athene?

ATHENE. Marriage does wonders.

GUY. Thanks.

ATHENE. Oh! Guy, don't be horrid. I feel awfully bad.

GUY. Well, what do you think I feel? "Cad!"

They turn to see ANNIE in hat and coat, with a suit-case in her hand, coming from the door Left.

ANNIE. Oh! ma'am, please, Miss, I want to go home.

GUY. [Exasperated!] She wants to go home—she wants to go home!

ATHENE. Guy! All right, Annie.

ANNIE. Oh! thank you, Miss. [She moves across in front of them].

ATHENE. [Suddenly] Annie!

ANNIE stops and turns to her.

What are you afraid of?

ANNIE. [With comparative boldness] I—I might catch it, Miss.

ATHENE. From your people?

ANNIE. Oh! no, Miss; from you. You see, I've got a young man that wants to marry me. And if I don't let him, I might get into trouble meself.

ATHENE. What sort of father and mother have you got, Annie?

ANNIE. I never thought, Miss. And of course I don't want to begin.

ATHENE. D'you mean you've never noticed how they treat each other?

ANNIE. I don't think they do, Miss.

ATHENE. Exactly.

ANNIE. They haven't time. Father's an engine driver.

GUY. And what's your young man, Annie?

ANNIE. [Embarrassed] Somethin' like you, sir. But very respectable.

ATHENE. And suppose you marry him, and he treats you like a piece of furniture?

ANNIE. I—I could treat him the same, Miss.

ATHENE. Don't you believe that, Annie!

ANNIE. He's very mild.

ATHENE. That's because he wants you. You wait till he doesn't.

ANNIE looks at GUY.

GUY. Don't you believe her, Annie; if he's decent—

ANNIE. Oh! yes, sir.

ATHENE. [Suppressing a smile] Of course—but the point is, Annie, that marriage makes all the difference.

ANNIE. Yes, Miss; that's what I thought.

ATHENE. You don't see. What I mean is that when once he's sure of you, he may change completely.

ANNIE. [Slowly, looking at her thumb] Oh! I don't—think—he'll hammer me, Miss. Of course, I know you can't tell till you've found out.

ATHENE. Well, I've no right to influence you.

ANNIE. Oh! no, Miss; that's what I've been thinking.

-GUY. You're quite right, Annie=-this is no place for you.

ANNIE. You see, we can't be married; sir, till he gets his rise. So it'll be a continual temptation to me.

ATHENE. Well, all right, Annie. I hope you'll never regret it.

ANNIE. Oh! no, Miss.

GUY. I say, Annie, don't go away thinking evil of us; we didn't realise you knew we weren't married.

ATHENE. We certainly did not.

ANNIE. Oh! I didn't think it right to take notice.

GUY. We beg your pardon.

ANNIE. Oh! no, sir. Only, seein' Mr and Mrs Builder so upset, brought it 'ome like. And father can be 'andy with a strap.

ATHENE. There you are! Force majeure!

ANNIE. Oh! yes, Miss.

ATHENE. Well, good-bye, Annie. What are you going to say to your people?

ANNIE. Oh! I shan't say I've been livin' in a family that wasn't a family, Miss. It wouldn't do no good.

ATHENE. Well, here are your wages.

ANNIE. Oh! I'm puttin' you out, Miss. [She takes the money].

ATHENE. Nonsense, Annie. And here's your fare home.

ANNIE. Oh! thank you, Miss. I'm very sorry. Of course if you was to change your mind [She stops, embarrassed].

ATHENE. I don't think—

GUY. [Abruptly] Good-bye, Annie. Here's five bob for the movies.

ANNIE. Oh! good-bye, sir, and thank you. I was goin' there now with my young man. He's just round the corner.

GUY. Be very careful of him.

ANNIE. Oh! yes, sir, I will. Good-bye, sir. Goodbye, Miss.

She goes.

GUY. So her father has a firm hand too. But it takes her back to the nest. How's that, Athene?

ATHENE. [Playing with a leathern button on his coat] If you'd watched it ever since you could watch anything, seen it kill out all—It's having power that does it. I know Father's got awfully good points.

GUY. Well, they don't stick out.

ATHENE. He works fearfully hard; he's upright, and plucky. He's not stingy. But he's smothered his animal nature-and that's done it. I don't want to see you smother anything, Guy.

GUY. [Gloomily] I suppose one never knows what one's got under the lid. If he hadn't come here to-day—[He spins the wedding ring] He certainly gives one pause. Used he to whack you?

ATHENE. Yes.

GUY. Brute!

ATHENE. With the best intentions. You see, he's a Town Councillor, and a magistrate. I suppose they have to be "firm." Maud and I sneaked in once to listen to him. There was a woman who came for protection from her husband. If he'd known we were there, he'd have had a fit.

GUY. Did he give her the protection?

ATHENE. Yes; he gave her back to the husband. Wasn't it—English?

GUY. [With a grunt] Hang it! We're not all like that.

ATHENE. [Twisting his button] I think it's really a sense of property so deep that they don't know they've got it. Father can talk about freedom like a—politician.

GUY. [Fitting the wedding ring on her finger] Well! Let's see how it looks, anyway.

ATHENE. Don't play with fire, Guy.

GUY. There's something in atavism, darling; there really is. I like it —I do.

A knock on the door.

ATHENE. That sounds like Annie again. Just see.

GUY. [Opening the door] It is. Come in, Annie. What's wrong now?

ANNIE. [Entering in confusion] Oh! sir, please, sir—I've told my young man.

ATHENE. Well, what does he say?

ANNIE. 'E was 'orrified, Miss.

GUY. The deuce he was! At our conduct?

ANNIE. Oh! no, sir—at mine.

ATHENE. But you did your best; you left us.

ANNIE. Oh! yes, Miss; that's why 'e's horrified.

GUY. Good for your young man.

ANNIE. [Flattered] Yes, sir. 'E said I 'ad no strength of mind.

ATHENE. So you want to come back?

ANNIE. Oh! yes, Miss.

ATHENE. All right.

GUY. But what about catching it?

ANNIE. Oh, sir, 'e said there was nothing like Epsom salts.

GUY. He's a wag, your young man.

ANNIE. He was in the Army, sir.

GUY. You said he was respectable.

ANNIE. Oh! yes, sir; but not so respectable as that.

ATHENE. Well, Annie, get your things off, and lay lunch.

ANNIE. Oh! yes, Miss.

She makes a little curtsey and passes through into the kitchen.

GUY. Strength of mind! Have a little, Athene won't you? [He holds out the marriage licence before her].

ATHENE. I don't know—I don't know! If—it turned out—

GUY. It won't. Come on. Must take chances in this life.

ATHENE. [Looking up into his face] Guy, promise me—solemnly that you'll never let me stand in your way, or stand in mine!

GUY. Right! That's a bargain. [They embrace.]

ATHENE quivers towards him. They embrace fervently as ANNIE enters with the bread pan. They spring apart.

ANNIE. Oh!

GUY. It's all right, Annie. There's only one more day's infection before you. We're to be married to-morrow morning.

ANNIE. Oh! yes, sir. Won't Mr Builder be pleased?

GUY. H'm! That's not exactly our reason.

ANNIE. [Right] Oh! no, sir. Of course you can't be a family without, can you?

GUY. What have you got in that thing?

ANNIE is moving across with the bread pan. She halts at the bedroom door.

ANNIE. Oh! please, ma'am, I was to give you a message—very important— from Miss Maud Builder "Lookout! Father is coming!"

She goes out. The CURTAIN falls.

## ACT II

BUILDER'S study. At the table, MAUD has just put a sheet of paper into a typewriter. She sits facing the audience, with her hands stretched over the keys.

MAUD. [To herself] I must get that expression.

Her face assumes a furtive, listening look. Then she gets up, whisks to the mirror over the fireplace, scrutinises the expression in it, and going back to the table, sits down again with hands outstretched above the keys, and an accentuation of the expression. The door up Left is opened, and TOPPING appears. He looks at MAUD, who just turns her eyes.

TOPPING. Lunch has been ready some time, Miss Maud.

MAUD. I don't want any lunch. Did you give it?

TOPPING. Miss Athene was out. I gave the message to a young party. She looked a bit green, Miss. I hope nothing'll go wrong with the works. Shall I keep lunch back?

MAUD. If something's gone wrong, they won't have any appetite, Topping.

TOPPING. If you think I might risk it, Miss, I'd like to slip round to my dentist. [He lays a finger on his cheek].

MAUD. [Smiling] Oh! What race is being run this afternoon, then, Topping?

TOPPING. [Twinkling, and shifting his finger to the side of his nose] Well, I don't suppose you've 'eard of it, Miss; but as a matter of fact it's the Cesarwitch.

MAUD. Got anything on?

TOPPING. Only my shirt, Miss.

MAUD. Is it a good thing, then?

TOPPING. I've seen worse roll up. [With a touch of enthusiasm] Dark horse, Miss Maud, at twenty to one.

MAUD. Put me ten bob on, Topping. I want all the money I can get, just now.

TOPPING. You're not the first, Miss.

MAUD. I say, Topping, do you know anything about the film?

TOPPING. [Nodding] Rather a specialty of mine, Miss.

MAUD. Well, just stand there, and give me your opinion of this.

TOPPING moves down Left. She crouches over the typewriter, lets her hands play on the keys; stops; assumes that listening, furtive look; listens again, and lets her head go slowly round, preceded by her eyes; breaks it off, and says:

What should you say I was?

TOPPING. Guilty, Miss.

MAUD. [With triumph] There! Then you think I've got it?

TOPPING. Well, of course, I couldn't say just what sort of a crime you'd committed, but I should think pretty 'ot stuff.

MAUD. Yes; I've got them here. [She pats her chest].

TOPPING. Really, Miss.

MAUD. Yes. There's just one point, Topping; it's psychological.

TOPPING. Indeed, Miss?

MAUD. Should I naturally put my hand on them; or would there be a reaction quick enough to stop me? You see, I'm alone—and the point is whether the fear of being seen would stop me although I knew I couldn't be seen. It's rather subtle.

TOPPING. I think there's be a rehaction, Miss.

MAUD. So do I. To touch them [She clasps her chest] is a bit obvious, isn't it?

TOPPING. If the haudience knows you've got 'em there.

MAUD. Oh! yes, it's seen me put them. Look here, I'll show you that too.

She opens an imaginary drawer, takes out some bits of sealing-wax, and with every circumstance of stealth in face and hands, conceals them in her bosom.

All right?

TOPPING. [Nodding] Fine, Miss. You have got a film face. What are they, if I may ask?

MAUD. [Reproducing the sealing-wax] The Fanshawe diamonds. There's just one thing here too, Topping.

In real life, which should I naturally do—put them in here [She touches her chest] or in my bag?

TOPPING. [Touching his waistcoat—earnestly] Well! To put 'em in here, Miss, I should say is more—more pishchological.

MAUD. [Subduing her lips] Yes; but—

TOPPING. You see, then you've got 'em on you.

MAUD. But that's just the point. Shouldn't I naturally think: Safer in my bag; then I can pretend somebody put them there. You see, nobody could put them on me.

TOPPING. Well, I should say that depends on your character. Of course I don't know what your character is.

MAUD. No; that's the beastly part of it—the author doesn't, either. It's all left to me.

TOPPING. In that case, I should please myself, Miss. To put 'em in 'ere's warmer.

MAUD. Yes, I think you're right. It's more human.

TOPPING. I didn't know you 'ad a taste this way, Miss Maud.

MAUD. More than a taste, Topping—a talent.

TOPPING. Well, in my belief, we all have a vice about us somewhere. But if I were you, Miss, I wouldn't touch bettin', not with this other on you. You might get to feel a bit crowded.

MAUD. Well, then, only put the ten bob on if you're sure he's going to win. You can post the money on after me. I'll send you an address, Topping, because I shan't be here.

TOPPING. [Disturbed] What! You're not going, too, Miss Maud?

MAUD. To seek my fortune.

TOPPING. Oh! Hang it all, Miss, think of what you'll leave behind. Miss Athene's leavin' home has made it pretty steep, but this'll touch bottom—this will.

MAUD. Yes; I expect you'll find it rather difficult for a bit when I'm gone. Miss Baldini, you know. I've been studying with her. She's got me this chance with the movie people. I'm going on trial as the guilty typist in "The Heartache of Miranda."

TOPPING. [Surprised out of politeness] Well, I never! That does sound like 'em! Are you goin' to tell the guv'nor, Miss?

MAUD nods. In that case, I think I'll be gettin' off to my dentist before the band plays.

MAUD. All right, Topping; hope you won't lose a tooth.

TOPPING. [With a grin] It's on the knees of the gods, Miss, as they say in the headlines.

He goes. MAUD stretches herself and listens.

MAUD. I believe that's them. Shivery funky.

She runs off up Left.

BUILDER. [Entering from the hall and crossing to the fireplace] Monstrous! Really monstrous!

CAMILLE enters from the hall. She has a little collecting book in her hand.

BUILDER. Well, Camille?

CAMILLE. A sistare from the Sacred 'Eart, Monsieur—her little book for the orphan children.

BUILDER. I can't be bothered—What is it?

CAMILLE. Orphan, Monsieur.

BUILDER. H'm! Well! [Feeling in his breast pocket] Give her that.

He hands her a five-pound note.

CAMILLE. I am sure she will be veree grateful for the poor little beggars. Madame says she will not be coming to lunch, Monsieur.

BUILDER. I don't want any, either. Tell Topping I'll have some coffee.

CAMILLE. Topping has gone to the dentist, Monsieur; 'e 'as the toothache.

BUILDER. Toothache—poor devil! H'm! I'm expecting my brother, but I don't know that I can see him.

CAMILLE. No, Monsieur?

BUILDER. Ask your mistress to come here.

He looks up, and catching her eye, looks away.

CAMILLE. Yes, Monsieur.

As she turns he looks swiftly at her, sweeping her up and down. She turns her head and catches his glance, which is swiftly dropped. Will Monsieur not 'ave anything to eat?

BUILDER. [Shaking his head-abruptly] No. Bring the coffee!

CAMILLE. Is Monsieur not well?

BUILDER. Yes—quite well.

CAMILLE. [Sweetening her eyes] A cutlet soubise? No?

BUILDER. [With a faint response in his eyes, instantly subdued] Nothing! nothing!

CAMILLE. And Madame nothing too—Tt! Tt! With her hand on the door she looks back, again catches his eyes in an engagement instantly broken off, and goes out.

BUILDER. [Stock-still, and staring at the door] That girl's a continual irritation to me! She's dangerous! What a life! I believe that girl—

The door Left is opened and MRS BUILDER comes in.

BUILDER. There's some coffee coming; do your head good. Look here, Julia. I'm sorry I beat on that door. I apologize. I was in a towering passion. I wish I didn't get into these rages. But—dash it all—! I couldn't walk away and leave you there.

MRS BUILDER. Why not?

BUILDER. You keep everything to yourself, so; I never have any notion what you're thinking. What did you say to her?

MRS BUILDER. Told her it would never work.

BUILDER. Well, that's something. She's crazy. D'you suppose she was telling the truth about that young blackguard wanting to marry her?

MRS BUILDER. I'm sure of it.

BUILDER. When you think of how she's been brought up. You would have thought that religion alone—

MRS BUILDER. The girls haven't wanted to go to church for years. They've always said they didn't see why they should go to keep up your position. I don't know if you remember that you once caned them for running off on a Sunday morning.

BUILDER. Well?

MRS BUILDER. They've never had any religion since.

BUILDER. H'm! [He takes a short turn up the room] What's to be done about Athene?

MRS BUILDER. You said you had done with her.

BUILDER. You know I didn't mean that. I might just as well have said I'd done with you! Apply your wits, Julia! At any moment this thing may come out. In a little town like this you can keep nothing dark. How can I take this nomination for Mayor?

MRS BUILDER. Perhaps Ralph could help.

BUILDER. What? His daughters have never done anything disgraceful, and his wife's a pattern.

MRS BUILDER. Yes; Ralph isn't at all a family man.

BUILDER. [Staring at her] I do wish you wouldn't turn things upside down in that ironical way. It isn't—English.

MRS BUILDER. I can't help having been born in Jersey.

BUILDER. No; I suppose it's in your blood. The French— [He stops short].

MRS BUILDER. Yes?

BUILDER. Very irritating sometimes to a plain Englishman—that's all.

MRS BUILDER. Shall I get rid of Camille?

BUILDER. [Staring at her, then dropping his glance] Camille? What's she got to do with it?

MRS BUILDER. I thought perhaps you found her irritating.

BUILDER. Why should I?

CAMILLE comes in from the dining-room with the coffee.

Put it there. I want some brandy, please.

CAMILLE. I bring it, Monsieur.

She goes back demurely into the dining-room.

BUILDER. Topping's got toothache, poor chap! [Pouring out the coffee] Can't you suggest any way of making Athene see reason? Think of the example! Maud will be kicking over next. I shan't be able to hold my head up here.

MRS BUILDER. I'm afraid I can't do that for you.

BUILDER. [Exasperated] Look here, Julia! That wretched girl said something to me about our life together. What—what's the matter with that?

MRS BUILDER. It is irritating.

BUILDER. Be explicit.

MRS BUILDER. We have lived together twenty-three years, John. No talk will change such things.

BUILDER. Is it a question of money? You can always have more. You know that. [MRS BUILDER smiles] Oh! don't smile like that; it makes me feel quite sick!

CAMILLE enters with a decanter and little glasses, from the dining-room.

CAMILLE. The brandy, sir. Monsieur Ralph Builder has just come.

MRS BUILDER. Ask him in, Camille.

CAMILLE. Yes, Madame.

She goes through the doorway into the hall. MRS BUILDER, following towards the door, meets RALPH BUILDER, a man rather older than BUILDER and of opposite build and manner. He has a pleasant, whimsical face and grizzled hair.

MRS BUILDER. John wants to consult you, Ralph.

RALPH. That's very gratifying.

She passes him and goes out, leaving the two brothers eyeing one another.

About the Welsh contract?

BUILDER. No. Fact is, Ralph, something very horrible's happened.

RALPH. Athene gone and got married?

BUILDER. No. It's, it's that she's gone and, and not got married.

RALPH utters a sympathetic whistle.

Jolly, isn't it?

RALPH. To whom?

BUILDER. A young flying bounder.

RALPH. And why?

BUILDER. Some crazy rubbish about family life, of all things.

RALPH. Athene's a most interesting girl. All these young people are so queer and delightful.

BUILDER. By George, Ralph, you may thank your stars you haven't got a delightful daughter. Yours are good, decent girls.

RALPH. Athene's tremendously good and decent, John. I'd bet any money she's doing this on the highest principles.

BUILDER. Behaving like a—

RALPH. Don't say what you'll regret, old man! Athene always took things seriously—bless her!

BUILDER. Julia thinks you might help. You never seem to have any domestic troubles.

RALPH. No—o. I don't think we do.

BUILDER. How d'you account for it?

RALPH. I must ask at home.

BUILDER. Dash it! You must know!

RALPH. We're all fond of each other.

BUILDER. Well, I'm fond of my girls too; I suppose I'm not amiable enough. H'm?

RALPH. Well, old man, you do get blood to the head. But what's Athene's point, exactly?

BUILDER. Family life isn't idyllic, so she thinks she and the young man oughtn't to have one.

RALPH. I see. Home experience?

BUILDER. Hang it all, a family's a family! There must be a head.

RALPH. But no tail, old chap.

BUILDER. You don't let your women folk do just as they like?

RALPH. Always.

BUILDER. What happens if one of your girls wants to do an improper thing? [RALPH shrugs his shoulders]. You don't stop her?

RALPH. Do you?

BUILDER. I try to.

RALPH. Exactly. And she does it. I don't and she doesn't.

BUILDER. [With a short laugh] Good Lord! I suppose you'd have me eat humble pie and tell Athene she can go on living in sin and offending society, and have my blessing to round it off.

RALPH. I think if you did she'd probably marry him.

BUILDER. You've never tested your theory, I'll bet.

RALPH. Not yet.

BUILDER. There you are.

RALPH. The 'suaviter in modo' pays, John. The times are not what they were.

BUILDER. Look here! I want to get to the bottom of this. Do you tell me I'm any stricter than nine out of ten men?

RALPH. Only in practice.

BUILDER. [Puzzled] How do you mean?

RALPH. Well, you profess the principles of liberty, but you practise the principles of government.

BUILDER. H'm! [Taking up the decanter] Have some?

RALPH. No, thank you.

BUILDER fills and raises his glass.

CAMILLE. [Entering] Madame left her coffee.

She comes forward, holds out a cup for BUILDER to pour into, takes it and goes out. BUILDER'S glass remains suspended. He drinks the brandy off as she shuts the door.

BUILDER. Life isn't all roses, Ralph.

RALPH. Sorry, old man.

BUILDER. I sometimes think I try myself too high. Well, about that Welsh contract?

RALPH. Let's take it.

BUILDER. If you'll attend to it. Frankly, I'm too upset.

As they go towards the door into the hall, MAUD comes in from the dining-room, in hat and coat.

RALPH. [Catching sight of her] Hallo! All well in your cosmogony, Maud?

MAUD. What is a cosmogony, Uncle?

RALPH. My dear, I—I don't know.

He goes out, followed by BUILDER. MAUD goes quickly to the table, sits down and rests her elbows on it, her chin on her hands, looking at the door.

BUILDER. [Re-entering] Well, Maud! You'd have won your bet!

MAUD. Oh! father, I—I've got some news for you.

BUILDER. [Staring at her] News—what?

MAUD. I'm awfully sorry, but I-I've got a job.

BUILDER. Now, don't go saying you're going in for Art, too, because I won't have it.

MAUD. Art? Oh! no! It's the—[With a jerk]—the Movies.

BUILDER. who has taken up a pipe to fill, puts it down.

BUILDER. [Impressively] I'm not in a joking mood.

MAUD. I'm not joking, father.

BUILDER. Then what are you talking about?

MAUD. You see, I—I've got a film face, and—

BUILDER. You've what? [Going up to his daughter, he takes hold of her chin] Don't talk nonsense! Your sister has just tried me to the limit.

MAUD. [Removing his hand from her chin] Don't oppose it, father, please! I've always wanted to earn my own living.

BUILDER. Living! Living!

MAUD. [Gathering determination] You can't stop me, father, because I shan't need support. I've got quite good terms.

BUILDER. [Almost choking, but mastering himself] Do you mean to say you've gone as far as that?

MAUD. Yes. It's all settled.

BUILDER. Who put you up to this?

MAUD. No one. I've been meaning to, ever so long. I'm twenty-one, you know.

BUILDER. A film face! Good God! Now, look here! I will not have a daughter of mine mixed up with the stage. I've spent goodness knows what on your education—both of you.

MAUD. I don't want to be ungrateful; but I—I can't go on living at home.

BUILDER. You can't—! Why? You've every indulgence.

MAUD. [Clearly and coldly] I can remember occasions when your indulgence hurt, father. [She wriggles her shoulders and back] We never forgot or forgave that.

BUILDER. [Uneasily] That! You were just kids.

MAUD. Perhaps you'd like to begin again?

BUILDER. Don't twist my tail, Maud. I had the most painful scene with Athene this morning. Now come! Give up this silly notion! It's really too childish!

MAUD. [Looking at him curiously] I've heard you say ever so many times that no man was any good who couldn't make his own way, father. Well, women are the same as men, now. It's the law of the country. I only want to make my own way.

BUILDER. [Trying to subdue his anger] Now, Maud, don't be foolish. Consider my position here—a Town Councillor, a Magistrate, and Mayor next year. With one daughter living with a man she isn't married to—

MAUD. [With lively interest] Oh! So you did catch them out?

BUILDER. D'you mean to say you knew?

MAUD. Of course.

BUILDER. My God! I thought we were a Christian family.

MAUD. Oh! father.

BUILDER. Don't sneer at Christianity!

MAUD. There's only one thing wrong with Christians—they aren't!

BUILDER Seizes her by the shoulders and shakes her vigorously. When he drops her shoulders, she gets up, gives him a vicious look, and suddenly stamps her foot on his toe with all her might.

BUILDER. [With a yowl of pain] You little devil!

MAUD. [Who has put the table between them] I won't stand being shaken.

BUILDER. [Staring at her across the table] You've got my temper up and you'll take the consequences. I'll make you toe the line.

MAUD. If you knew what a Prussian expression you've got!

BUILDER passes his hand across his face uneasily, as if to wipe something off.

No! It's too deep!

BUILDER. Are you my daughter or are you not?

MAUD. I certainly never wanted to be. I've always disliked you, father, ever since I was so high. I've seen through you. Do you remember when you used to come into the nursery because Jenny was pretty? You think we didn't notice that, but we did. And in the schoolroom—Miss Tipton. And d'you remember knocking our heads together? No, you don't; but we do. And—

BUILDER. You disrespectful monkey! Will you be quiet?

MAUD. No; you've got to hear things. You don't really love anybody but yourself, father. What's good for you has to be good for everybody. I've often heard you talk about independence, but it's a limited company and you've got all the shares.

BUILDER. Rot; only people who can support themselves have a right to independence.

MAUD. That's why you don't want me to support myself.

BUILDER. You can't! Film, indeed! You'd be in the gutter in a year. Athene's got her pittance, but you—you've got nothing.

MAUD. Except my face.

BUILDER. It's the face that brings women to ruin, my girl.

MAUD. Well, when I'm there I won't come to you to rescue me.

BUILDER. Now, mind—if you leave my house, I've done with you.

MAUD. I'd rather scrub floors now, than stay.

BUILDER. [Almost pathetically] Well, I'm damned! Look here, Maud— all this has been temper. You got my monkey up. I'm sorry I shook you; you've had your revenge on my toes. Now, come! Don't make things worse for me than they are. You've all the liberty you can reasonably want till you marry.

MAUD. He can't see it—he absolutely can't!

BUILDER. See what?

MAUD. That I want to live a life of my own.

He edges nearer to her, and she edges to keep her distance.

BUILDER. I don't know what's bitten you.

MAUD. The microbe of freedom; it's in the air.

BUILDER. Yes, and there it'll stay—that's the first sensible word you've uttered. Now, come! Take your hat off, and let's be friends!

MAUD looks at him and slowly takes off her hat.

BUILDER. [Relaxing his attitude, with a sigh of relief] That's right! [Crosses to fireplace].

MAUD. [Springing to the door leading to the hall] Good-bye, father!

BUILDER. [Following her] Monkey!

At the sound of a bolt shot, BUILDER goes up to the window. There is a fumbling at the door, and CAMILLE appears.

BUILDER. What's the matter with that door? CAMILLE. It was bolted, Monsieur.

BUILDER. Who bolted it?

CAMILLE. [Shrugging her shoulders] I can't tell, Monsieur.

She collects the cups, and halts close to him. [Softly] Monsieur is not 'appy.

BUILDER. [Surprised] What? No! Who'd be happy in a household like mine?

CAMILLE. But so strong a man—I wish I was a strong man, not a weak woman.

BUILDER. [Regarding her with reluctant admiration] Why, what's the matter with you?

CAMILLE. Will Monsieur have another glass of brandy before I take it?

BUILDER. No! Yes—I will.

She pours it out, and he drinks it, hands her the glass and sits down suddenly in an armchair. CAMILLE puts the glass on a tray, and looks for a box of matches from the mantelshelf.

CAMILLE. A light, Monsieur?

BUILDER. Please.

CAMILLE. [She trips over his feet and sinks on to his knee] Oh! Monsieur!

BUILDER flames up and catches her in his arms

Oh! Monsieur—

BUILDER. You little devil!

She suddenly kisses him, and he returns the kiss. While they are engaged in this entrancing occupation, MRS BUILDER opens the door from the hall, watches unseen for a few seconds, and quietly goes out again.

BUILDER. [Pushing her back from him, whether at the sound of the door or of a still small voice] What am I doing?

CAMILLE. Kissing.

BUILDER. I—I forgot myself.

They rise.

CAMILLE. It was na-ice.

BUILDER. I didn't mean to. You go away—go away!

CAMILLE. Oh! Monsieur, that spoil it.

BUILDER. [Regarding her fixedly] It's my opinion you're a temptation of the devil. You know you sat down on purpose.

CAMILLE. Well, perhaps.

BUILDER. What business had you to? I'm a family man.

CAMILLE. Yes. What a pity! But does it matter?

BUILDER. [Much beset] Look here, you know! This won't do! It won't do! I—I've got my reputation to think of!

CAMILLE. So 'ave I! But there is lots of time to think of it in between.

BUILDER. I knew you were dangerous. I always knew it.

CAMILLE. What a thing to say of a little woman!

BUILDER. We're not in Paris.

CAMILLE. [Clasping her hands] Oh! 'Ow I wish we was!

BUILDER. Look here—I can't stand this; you've got to go. Out with you! I've always kept a firm hand on myself, and I'm not going to—

CAMILLE. But I admire you so!

BUILDER. Suppose my wife had come in?

CAMILLE. Oh! Don't suppose any such a disagreeable thing! If you were not so strict, you would feel much 'appier.

BUILDER. [Staring at her] You're a temptress!

CAMILLE. I lofe pleasure, and I don't get any. And you 'ave such a duty, you don't get any sport. Well, I am 'ere!

She stretches herself, and BUILDER utters a deep sound.

BUILDER. [On the edge of succumbing] It's all against my—I won't do it! It's—it's wrong!

CAMILLE. Oh! La, la!

BUILDER. [Suddenly revolting] No! If you thought it a sin—I—might. But you don't; you're nothing but a—a little heathen.

CAMILLE. Why should it be better if I thought it a sin?

BUILDER. Then—then I should know where I was. As it is—

CAMILLE. The English 'ave no idea of pleasure. They make it all so coarse and virtuous.

BUILDER. Now, out you go before I—! Go on!

He goes over to the door and opens it. His wife is outside in a hat and coat. She comes in.

[Stammering] Oh! Here you are—I wanted you.

CAMILLE, taking up the tray, goes out Left, swinging her hips a very little.

BUILDER. Going out?

MRS BUILDER. Obviously.

BUILDER. Where?

MRS BUILDER. I don't know at present.

BUILDER. I wanted to talk to you about Maud.

MRS BUILDER. It must wait.

BUILDER. She's-she's actually gone and—

MRS BUILDER. I must tell you that I happened to look in a minute ago.

BUILDER. [In absolute dismay] You! You what?

MRS BUILDER. Yes. I will put no obstacle in the way of your pleasures.

BUILDER. [Aghast] Put no obstacle? What do you mean? Julia, how can you say a thing like that? Why, I've only just—

MRS BUILDER. Don't! I saw.

BUILDER. The girl fell on my knees. Julia, she did. She's—she's a little devil. I—I resisted her. I give you my word there's been nothing beyond a kiss, under great provocation. I—I apologise.

MRS BUILDER. [Bows her head] Thank you! I quite understand. But you must forgive my feeling it impossible to remain a wet blanket any longer.

BUILDER. What! Because of a little thing like that—all over in two minutes, and I doing my utmost.

MRS BUILDER. My dear John, the fact that you had to do your utmost is quite enough. I feel continually humiliated in your house, and I want to leave it—quite quietly, without fuss of any kind.

BUILDER. But—my God! Julia, this is awful—it's absurd! How can you? I'm your husband. Really— your saying you don't mind what I do—it's not right; it's immoral!

MRS BUILDER. I'm afraid you don't see what goes on in those who live with you. So, I'll just go. Don't bother!

BUILDER. Now, look here, Julia, you can't mean this seriously. You can't! Think of my position! You've never set yourself up against me before.

MRS BUILDER. But I do now.

BUILDER. [After staring at her] I've given you no real reason. I'll send the girl away. You ought to thank me for resisting a temptation that most men would have yielded to. After twenty-three years of married life, to kick up like this—you ought to be ashamed of yourself.

MRS BUILDER. I'm sure you must think so.

BUILDER. Oh! for heaven's sake don't be sarcastic! You're my wife, and there's an end of it; you've no legal excuse. Don't be absurd!

MRS BUILDER. Good-bye!

BUILDER. D'you realise that you're encouraging me to go wrong? That's a pretty thing for a wife to do. You ought to keep your husband straight.

MRS BUILDER. How beautifully put!

BUILDER. [Almost pathetically] Don't rile me Julia! I've had an awful day. First Athene—then Maud—then that girl—and now you! All at once like this! Like a swarm of bees about one's head. [Pleading] Come, now, Julia, don't be so—so im practicable! You'll make us the laughing-stock of the whole town. A man in my position, and can't keep his own family; it's preposterous!

MRS BUILDER. Your own family have lives and thoughts and feelings of their own.

BUILDER. Oh! This damned Woman's business! I knew how it would be when we gave you the vote. You and I are married, and our daughters are our daughters. Come, Julia. Where's your commonsense? After twenty-three years! You know I can't do without you!

MRS BUILDER. You could—quite easily. You can tell people what you like.

BUILDER. My God! I never heard anything so immoral in all my life from the mother of two grownup girls. No wonder they've turned out as they have! What is it you want, for goodness sake?

MRS BUILDER. We just want to be away from you, that's all. I assure you it's best. When you've shown some consideration for our feelings and some real sign that we exist apart from you—we could be friends again— perhaps—I don't know.

BUILDER. Friends! Good heavens! With one's own wife and daughters! [With great earnestness] Now, look here, Julia, you haven't lived with me all this time without knowing that I'm a man of strong passions; I've been a faithful husband to you—yes, I have. And that means resisting all sorts of temptations you know nothing of. If you withdraw from my society I won't answer for the consequences. In fact, I can't have you withdrawing. I'm not going to see myself going to the devil and losing the good opinion of everybody round me. A bargain's a bargain. And until I've broken my side of it, and I tell you I haven't—you've no business to break yours. That's flat. So now, put all that out of your head.

MRS BUILDER. No.

BUILDER. [Intently] D'you realise that I've supported you in luxury and comfort?

MRS BUILDER. I think I've earned it.

BUILDER. And how do you propose to live? I shan't give you a penny. Come, Julia, don't be such an idiot! Fancy letting a kiss which no man could have helped, upset you like this!

MRS BUILDER. The Camille, and the last straw!

BUILDER. [Sharply] I won't have it. So now you know.

But MRS BUILDER has very swiftly gone.

Julia, I tell you— [The outer door is heard being closed] Damnation! I will not have it! They're all mad! Here—where's my hat?

He looks distractedly round him, wrenches open the door, and a moment later the street door is heard to shut with a bang.

CURTAIN.

**ACT III**

**SCENE I**

Ten o'clock the following morning, in the study of the Mayor of Breconridge, a panelled room with no window visible, a door Left back and a door Right forward. The entire back wall is furnished with books from floor to ceiling; the other walls are panelled and bare. Before the fireplace, Left, are two armchairs, and other chairs are against the walls. On the Right is a writing-bureau at right angles to the footlights, with a chair behind it. At its back corner stands HARRIS, telephoning.

HARRIS. What—[Pause] Well, it's infernally awkward, Sergeant.... The Mayor's in a regular stew.... [Listens] New constable? I should think so! Young fool! Look here, Martin, the only thing to do is to hear the charge here at once. I've sent for Mr Chantrey; he's on his way. Bring Mr Builder and the witnesses round sharp. See? And, I say, for God's sake keep it dark. Don't let the Press get on to it. Why you didn't let him go home—! Black eye? The constable? Well, serve him right. Blundering young ass! I mean, it's undermining all authority.... Well, you oughtn't—at least, I... Damn it all!—it's a nine days' wonder if it gets out—! All right! As soon as you can. [He hangs up the receiver, puts a second chair behind the bureau, and other chairs facing it.] [To himself] Here's a mess! Johnny Builder, of all men! What price Mayors!

The telephone rings.

Hallo?... Poaching charge? Well, bring him too; only, I say, keep him back till the other's over. By the way, Mr Chantrey's going shooting. He'll want to get off by eleven. What?.. Righto!

As he hangs up the receiver the MAYOR enters. He looks worried, and is still dressed with the indefinable wrongness of a burgher.

MAYOR. Well, 'Arris?

HARRIS. They'll be over in five minutes, Mr Mayor.

MAYOR. Mr Chantrey?

HARRIS. On his way, sir.

MAYOR. I've had some awkward things to deal with in my time, 'Arris, but this is just about the [Sniffs] limit.

HARRIS. Most uncomfortable, Sir; most uncomfortable!

MAYOR. Put a book on the chair, 'Arris; I like to sit 'igh.

HARRIS puts a volume of Encyclopaedia on the Mayor's chair behind the bureau.

[Deeply] Our fellow-magistrate! A family man! In my shoes next year. I suppose he won't be, now. You can't keep these things dark.

HARRIS. I've warned Martin, sir, to use the utmost discretion. Here's Mr Chantrey.

By the door Left, a pleasant and comely gentleman has entered, dressed with indefinable rightness in shooting clothes.

MAYOR. Ah, Chantrey!

CHANTREY. How de do, Mr Mayor? [Nodding to HARRIS] This is extraordinarily unpleasant.

The MAYOR nods.

What on earth's he been doing?

HARRIS. Assaulting one of his own daughters with a stick; and resisting the police.

CHANTREY. [With a low whistle] Daughter! Charity begins at home.

HARRIS. There's a black eye.

MAYOR. Whose?

HARRIS. The constable's.

CHANTREY. How did the police come into it?

HARRIS. I don't know, sir. The worst of it is he's been at the police station since four o'clock yesterday. The Superintendent's away, and Martin never will take responsibility.

CHANTREY. By George! he will be mad. John Builder's a choleric fellow.

MAYOR. [Nodding] He is. 'Ot temper, and an 'igh sense of duty.

HARRIS. There's one other charge, Mr Mayor—poaching. I told them to keep that back till after.

CHANTREY. Oh, well, we'll make short work of that. I want to get off by eleven, Harris. I shall be late for the first drive anyway. John Builder! I say, Mayor—but for the grace of God, there go we!

MAYOR. Harris, go out and bring them in yourself; don't let the servants—

HARRIS goes out Left. The MAYOR takes the upper chair behind the bureau, sitting rather higher because of the book than CHANTREY, who takes the lower. Now that they are in the seats of justice, a sort of reticence falls on them, as if they were afraid of giving away their attitudes of mind to some unseen presence.

MAYOR. [Suddenly] H'm!

CHANTREY. Touch of frost. Birds ought to come well to the guns—no wind. I like these October days.

MAYOR. I think I 'ear them. H'm.

CHANTREY drops his eyeglass and puts on a pair of "grandfather" spectacles. The MAYOR clears his throat and takes up a pen. They neither of them look up as the door is opened and a little procession files in. First HARRIS; then RALPH BUILDER, ATHENE, HERRINGHAME, MAUD, MRS BUILDER, SERGEANT MARTIN, carrying a heavy Malacca cane with a silver knob; JOHN BUILDER and the CONSTABLE MOON, a young man with one black eye. No funeral was ever attended by mutes so solemn and dejected. They stand in a sort of row.

MAYOR. [Without looking up] Sit down, ladies; sit down.

HARRIS and HERRINGHAME succeed in placing the three women in chairs. RALPH BUILDER also sits. HERRINGHAME stands behind. JOHN BUILDER remains standing between the two POLICEMEN. His face is unshaved and menacing, but he stands erect staring straight at the MAYOR. HARRIS goes to the side of the bureau, Back, to take down the evidence.

MAYOR. Charges!

SERGEANT. John Builder, of The Cornerways, Breconridge, Contractor and Justice of the Peace, charged with assaulting his daughter Maud Builder by striking her with a stick in the presence of Constable Moon and two other persons; also with resisting Constable Moon in the execution of his duty, and injuring his eye. Constable Moon!

MOON. [Stepping forward-one, two—like an automaton, and saluting] In River Road yesterday afternoon, Your Worship, about three-thirty p.m., I was attracted by a young woman callin' "Constable" outside a courtyard. On hearing the words "Follow me, quick," I followed her to a painter's studio inside the courtyard, where I found three persons in the act of disagreement. No sooner 'ad I appeared than the defendant, who was engaged in draggin' a woman towards the door, turns to the young woman who accompanied me, with violence. "You dare, father," she says; whereupon he hit her twice with the stick the same which is produced, in the presence of myself and the two other persons, which I'm given to understand is his wife and other daughter.

MAYOR. Yes; never mind what you're given to understand.

MOON. No, sir. The party struck turns to me and says, "Come in. I give this man in charge for assault." I moves accordingly with the words: "I saw you. Come along with me." The defendant turns to me sharp and says: "You stupid lout—I'm a magistrate." "Come off it," I says to the best of my recollection. "You struck this woman in my presence," I says, "and you come along!" We were then at close quarters. The defendant gave me a push with the words: "Get out, you idiot!" "Not at all," I replies, and took 'old of his arm. A struggle ensues, in the course of which I receives the black eye which I herewith produce. [He touches his eye with awful solemnity.]

The MAYOR clears his throat; CHANTREY'S eyes goggle; HARRIS bends over and writes rapidly.

During the struggle, Your Worship, a young man has appeared on the scene, and at the instigation of the young woman, the same who was assaulted, assists me in securing the prisoner, whose language and resistance was violent in the extreme. We placed him in a cab which we found outside, and I conveyed him to the station.

CHANTREY. What was his—er—conduct in the—er—cab?

MOON. He sat quiet.

CHANTREY. That seems—

MOON. Seein' I had his further arm twisted behind him.

MAYOR [Looking at BUILDER] Any questions to ask him?

BUILDER makes not the faintest sign, and the MAYOR drops his glance.

MAYOR. Sergeant?

MOON steps back two paces, and the SERGEANT steps two paces forward.

SERGEANT. At ten minutes to four, Your Worship, yesterday afternoon, Constable Moon brought the defendant to the station in a four-wheeled cab. On his recounting the circumstances of the assault, they were taken down and read over to the defendant with the usual warning. The defendant said nothing. In view of the double assault and the condition of the constable's eye, and in the absence of the Superintendent, I thought it my duty to retain the defendant for the night.

MAYOR. The defendant said nothing?

SERGEANT. He 'as not opened his lips to my knowledge, Your Worship, from that hour to this.

MAYOR. Any questions to ask the Sergeant?

BUILDER continues to stare at the MAYOR without a word.

MAYOR. Very well!

The MAYOR and CHANTREY now consult each other inaudibly, and the Mayor nods.

MAYOR. Miss Maud Builder, will you tell us what you know of this, er, occurrence?

MAUD. [Rising; with eyes turning here and there] Must I?

MAYOR. I'm afraid you must.

MAUD. [After a look at her father, who never turns his eyes from the MAYOR's face] I—I wish to withdraw the charge of striking me, please. I—I never meant to make it. I was in a temper—I saw red.

MAYOR. I see. A—a domestic disagreement. Very well, that charge is withdrawn. You do not appear to have been hurt, and that seems to me quite proper. Now, tell me what you know of the assault on the constable. Is his account correct?

MAUD. [Timidly] Ye-yes. Only—

MAYOR. Yes? Tell us the truth.

MAUD. [Resolutely] Only, I don't think my father hit the constable. I think the stick did that.

.

MAYOR. Oh, the stick? But—er—the stick was in 'is 'and, wasn't it?

MAUD. Yes; but I mean, my father saw red, and the constable saw red, and the stick flew up between them and hit him in the eye.

CHANTREY. And then he saw black?

MAYOR. [With corrective severity] But did 'e 'it 'im with the stick?

MAUD. No—no. I don't think he did.

MAYOR. Then who supplied the—er—momentum?

MAUD. I think there was a struggle for the cane, and it flew up.

MAYOR. Hand up the cane.

The SERGEANT hands up the cane. The MAYOR and CHANTREY examine it. MAYOR. Which end—do you suggest—inflicted this injury?

MAUD. Oh! the knob end, sir.

MAYOR. What do you say to that, constable?

MOON. [Stepping the mechanical two paces] I don't deny there was a struggle, Your Worship, but it's my impression I was 'it.

CHANTREY. Of course you were bit; we can see that. But with the cane or with the fist?

MOON. [A little flurried] I—I—with the fist, sir.

MAYOR. Be careful. Will you swear to that?

MOON. [With that sudden uncertainty which comes over the most honest in such circumstances] Not—not so to speak in black and white, Your Worship; but that was my idea at the time.

MAYOR. You won't swear to it?

MOON. I'll swear he called me an idiot and a lout; the words made a deep impression on me.

CHANTREY. [To himself] Mort aux vaches!

MAYOR. Eh? That'll do, constable; stand back. Now, who else saw the struggle? Mrs Builder. You're not obliged to say anything unless you like. That's your privilege as his wife.

While he is speaking the door has been opened, and HARRIS has gone swiftly to it, spoken to someone and returned. He leans forward to the MAYOR.

Eh? Wait a minute. Mrs Builder, do you wish to give evidence?

MRS BUILDER. [Rising] No, Mr Mayor.

MRS BUILDER Sits.

MAYOR. Very good. [To HARRIS] Now then, what is it?

HARRIS says something in a low and concerned voice. The MAYOR'S face lengthens. He leans to his right and consults CHANTREY, who gives a faint and deprecating shrug. A moment's silence.

MAYOR. This is an open Court. The Press have the right to attend if they wish.

HARRIS goes to the door and admits a young man in glasses, of a pleasant appearance, and indicates to him a chair at the back. At this untimely happening BUILDER's eyes have moved from side to side, but now he regains his intent and bull-like stare at his fellow-justices.

MAYOR. [To Maud] You can sit down, Miss Builder.

MAUD resumes her seat.

Miss Athene Builder, you were present, I think?

ATHENE. [Rising] Yes, Sir.

MAYOR. What do you say to this matter?

ATHENE. I didn't see anything very clearly, but I think my sister's account is correct, sir.

MAYOR. Is it your impression that the cane inflicted the injury?

ATHENE. [In a low voice] Yes.

MAYOR. With or without deliberate intent?

ATHENE. Oh! without.

BUILDER looks at her.

MAYOR. But you were not in a position to see very well?

ATHENE. No, Sir.

MAYOR. Your sister having withdrawn her charge, we needn't go into that. Very good!

He motions her to sit down. ATHENE, turning her eyes on her Father's impassive figure, sits.

MAYOR. Now, there was a young man. [Pointing to HERRINGHAME] Is this the young man?

MOON. Yes, Your Worship.

MAYOR. What's your name?

GUY. Guy Herringhame.

MAYOR. Address?

GUY. Er—the Aerodrome, Sir. MAYOR. Private, I mean?

The moment is one of considerable tension.

GUY. [With an effort] At the moment, sir, I haven't one. I've just left my diggings, and haven't yet got any others.

MAYOR. H'm! The Aerodrome. How did you come to be present?

GUY. I—er

BUILDER's eyes go round and rest on him for a moment.

It's in my sister's studio that Miss Athene Builder is at present working, sir. I just happened to—to turn up.

MAYOR. Did you appear on the scene, as the constable says, during the struggle?

GUY. Yes, sir.

MAYOR. Did he summon you to his aid?

GUY. Yes—No, sir. Miss Maud Builder did that.

MAYOR. What do you say to this blow?

GUY. [Jerking his chin up a little] Oh! I saw that clearly.

MAYOR. Well, let us hear.

GUY. The constable's arm struck the cane violently and it flew up and landed him in the eye.

MAYOR. [With a little grunt] You are sure of that?

GUY. Quite sure, sir.

MAYOR. Did you hear any language?

GUY. Nothing out of the ordinary, sir. One or two damns and blasts.

MAYOR. You call that ordinary?

GUY. Well, he's a magistrate, sir.

The MAYOR utters a profound grunt. CHANTREY smiles. There is a silence. Then the MAYOR leans over to CHANTREY for a short colloquy.

CHANTREY. Did you witness any particular violence other than a resistance to arrest?

GUY. No, sir.

MAYOR. [With a gesture of dismissal] Very well, That seems to be the evidence. Defendant John Builder—what do you say to all this?

BUILDER. [In a voice different from any we have heard from him] Say! What business had he to touch me, a magistrate? I gave my daughter two taps with a cane in a private house, for interfering with me for taking my wife home—

MAYOR. That charge is not pressed, and we can't go into the circumstances. What do you wish to say about your conduct towards the constable?

BUILDER. [In his throat] Not a damned thing!

MAYOR. [Embarrassed] I—I didn't catch.

CHANTREY. Nothing—nothing, he said, Mr Mayor.

MAYOR. [Clearing his throat] I understand, then, that you do not wish to offer any explanation?

BUILDER. I consider myself abominably treated, and I refuse to say another word.

MAYOR. [Drily] Very good. Miss Maud Builder.

MAUD stands up.

MAYOR. When you spoke of the defendant seeing red, what exactly did you mean?

MAUD. I mean that my father was so angry that he didn't know what he was doing.

CHANTREY. Would you say as angry as he, er, is now?

MAUD. [With a faint smile] Oh! much more angry.

RALPH BUILDER stands up.

RALPH. Would you allow me to say a word, Mr Mayor?

MAYOR. Speaking of your own knowledge, Mr Builder?

RALPH. In regard to the state of my brother's mind—yes, Mr Mayor. He was undoubtedly under great strain yesterday; certain circumstances, domestic and otherwise—

MAYOR. You mean that he might have been, as one might say, beside himself?

RALPH. Exactly, Sir.

MAYOR. Had you seen your brother?

RALPH. I had seen him shortly before this unhappy business.

The MAYOR nods and makes a gesture, so that MAUD and RALPH sit down; then, leaning over, he confers in a low voice with CHANTREY. The rest all sit or stand exactly as if each was the only person in the room, except the JOURNALIST, who is writing busily and rather obviously making a sketch of BUILDER.

MAYOR. Miss Athene Builder.

ATHENE stands up.

This young man, Mr Herringhame, I take it, is a friend of the family's?

A moment of some tension.

ATHENE. N—no, Mr Mayor, not of my father or mother.

CHANTREY. An acquaintance of yours?

ATHENE. Yes.

MAYOR. Very good. [He clears his throat] As the defendant, wrongly, we think, refuses to offer his explanation of this matter, the Bench has to decide on the evidence as given. There seems to be some discrepancy as to the blow which the constable undoubtedly received. In view of this, we incline to take the testimony of Mr—

HARRIS prompts him.

Mr 'Erringhame—as the party least implicated personally in the affair, and most likely to 'ave a cool and impartial view. That evidence is to the effect that the blow was accidental. There is no doubt, however, that the defendant used reprehensible language, and offered some resistance to the constable in the execution of his duty. Evidence 'as been offered that he was in an excited state of mind; and it is possible —I don't say that this is any palliation—but it is possible that he may have thought his position as magistrate made him—er—

CHANTREY. [Prompting] Caesar's wife.

MAYOR. Eh? We think, considering all the circumstances, and the fact that he has spent a night in a cell, that justice will be met by—er—discharging him with a caution.

BUILDER. [With a deeply muttered] The devil you do!

Walks out of the room. The JOURNALIST, grabbing his pad, starts up and follows. The BUILDERS rise and huddle, and, with HERRINGHAME, are ushered out by HARRIS.

MAYOR. [Pulling out a large handkerchief and wiping his forehead] My Aunt!

CHANTREY. These new constables, Mayor! I say, Builder'll have to go! Damn the Press, how they nose everything out! The Great Unpaid! We shall get it again! [He suddenly goes off into a fit of laughter] "Come off it," I says, "to the best of my recollection." Oh! Oh! I shan't hit a bird all day! That poor devil Builder! It's no joke for him. You did it well, Mayor; you did it well. British justice is safe in your hands. He blacked the fellow's eye all right. "Which I herewith produce." Oh! my golly! It beats the band!

His uncontrollable laughter and the MAYOR'S rueful appreciation are exchanged with lightning rapidity for a preternatural solemnity, as the door opens, admitting SERGEANT MARTIN and the lugubrious object of their next attentions.

MAYOR. Charges.

SERGEANT steps forward to read the charge as The CURTAIN falls.


## SCENE II

Noon the same day. BUILDER'S study. TOPPING is standing by the open window, looking up and down the street. A newspaper boy's voice is heard calling the first edition of his wares. It approaches from the Right.

TOPPING. Here!

BOY'S VOICE. Right, guv'nor! Johnny Builder up before the beaks! [A paper is pushed up].

TOPPING. [Extending a penny] What's that you're sayin'? You take care!

BOY'S VOICE. It's all 'ere. Johnny Builder—beatin' his wife! Dischawged.

TOPPING. Stop it, you young limb!

BOY'S VOICE. 'Allo! What's the matter wiv you? Why, it's Johnny Builder's house! [Gives a cat-call] 'Ere, buy anuvver! 'E'll want to read about 'isself. [Appealing] Buy anuvver, guv'nor!

TOPPING. Move on!

He retreats from the window, opening the paper.

BOY'S VOICE. [Receding] Payper! First edition! J.P. chawged! Payper!

TOPPING. [To himself as he reads] Crimes! Phew! That accounts for them bein' away all night.

While he is reading, CAMILLE enters from the hall. Here! Have you seen this, Camel—in the Stop Press?

CAMILLE. No.

They read eagerly side by side.

TOPPING. [Finishing aloud] "Tried to prevent her father from forcing her mother to return home with him, and he struck her for so doing. She did not press the charge. The arrested gentleman, who said he acted under great provocation, was discharged with a caution." Well, I'm blowed! He has gone and done it!

CAMILLE. A black eye!

TOPPING. [Gazing at her] Have you had any hand in this? I've seen you making your lovely black eyes at him. You foreigners—you're a loose lot!

CAMILLE. You are drunk!

TOPPING. Not yet, my dear. [Reverting to the paper; philosophically] Well, this little lot's bust up! The favourites will fall down. Johnny Builder! Who'd have thought it?

CAMILLE. He is an obstinate man.

TOPPING. Ah! He's right up against it now. Comes of not knowin' when to stop bein' firm. If you meet a wall with your 'ead, it's any odds on the wall, Camel. Though, if you listened to some, you wouldn't think it. What'll he do now, I wonder? Any news of the mistress?

CAMILLE. [Shaking her head] I have pack her tr-runks.

TOPPING. Why?

CAMILLE. Because she take her jewels yesterday.

TOPPING. Deuce she did! They generally leave 'em. Take back yer gifts! She throws the baubles at 'is 'ead. [Again staring at her] You're a deep one, you know!

There is the sound of a cab stopping.

Wonder if that's him! [He goes towards the hall. CAMILLE watchfully shifts towards the diningroom door. MAUD enters.]

MAUD. Is my father back, Topping?

TOPPING. Not yet, Miss.

MAUD. I've come for mother's things.

CAMILLE. They are r-ready.

MAUD. [Eyeing her] Topping, get them down, please.

TOPPING, after a look at them both, goes out into the hall.

Very clever of you to have got them ready.

CAMILLE. I am clevare.

MAUD. [Almost to herself] Yes—father may, and he may not.

CAMILLE. Look! If you think I am a designing woman, you are mistook. I know when things are too 'ot. I am not sorry to go.

MAUD. Oh! you are going?

CAMILLE. Yes, I am going. How can I stay when there is no lady in the 'ouse?

MAUD. Not even if you're asked to?

CAMILLE. Who will ask me?

MAUD. That we shall see.

CAMILLE. Well, you will see I have an opinion of my own.

MAUD. Oh! yes, you're clear-headed enough.

CAMILLE. I am not arguing. Good-morning!

Exits up Left.

MAUD regards her stolidly as she goes out into the dining-room, then takes up the paper and reads.

MAUD. Horrible!

TOPPING re-enters from the hall.

TOPPING. I've got 'em on the cab, Miss. I didn't put your ten bob on yesterday, because the animal finished last. You can't depend on horses.

MAUD. [Touching the newspaper] This is a frightful business, Topping.

TOPPING. Ah! However did it happen, Miss Maud?

MAUD. [Tapping the newspaper] It's all true. He came after my mother to Miss Athene's, and I—I couldn't stand it. I did what it says here; and now I'm sorry. Mother's dreadfully upset. You know father as well as anyone, Topping; what do you think he'll do now?

TOPPING. [Sucking in his cheeks] Well, you see, Miss, it's like this: Up to now Mr Builder's always had the respect of everybody—

MAUD moves her head impatiently.

outside his own house, of course. Well, now he hasn't got it. Pishchologically that's bound to touch him.

MAUD. Of course; but which way? Will he throw up the sponge, or try and stick it out here?

TOPPING. He won't throw up the sponge, Miss; more likely to squeeze it down the back of their necks.

MAUD. He'll be asked to resign, of course.

The NEWSPAPER BOY'S VOICE is heard again approaching: "First edition! Great sensation! Local magistrate before the Bench! Pay-per!"

Oh, dear! I wish I hadn't! But I couldn't see mother being—

TOPPING. Don't you fret, Miss; he'll come through. His jaw's above his brow, as you might say.

MAUD. What?

TOPPING. [Nodding] Phreenology, Miss. I rather follow that. When the jaw's big and the brow is small, it's a sign of character. I always think the master might have been a Scotchman, except for his fishionomy.

MAUD. A Scotsman?

TOPPING. So down on anything soft, Miss. Haven't you noticed whenever one of these 'Umanitarians writes to the papers, there's always a Scotchman after him next morning. Seems to be a fact of 'uman nature, like introducin' rabbits into a new country and then weasels to get rid of 'em. And then something to keep down the weasels. But I never can see what could keep down a Scotchman! You seem to reach the hapex there!

MAUD. Miss Athene was married this morning, Topping. We've just come from the Registrar's.

TOPPING. [Immovably] Indeed, Miss. I thought perhaps she was about to be.

MAUD. Oh!

TOPPING. Comin' events. I saw the shadder yesterday.

MAUD. Well, it's all right. She's coming on here with my uncle.

A cab is heard driving up.

That's them, I expect. We all feel awful about father.

TOPPING. Ah! I shouldn't be surprised if he feels awful about you, Miss.

MAUD. [At the window] It is them.

TOPPING goes out into the hall; ATHENE and RALPH enter Right.

MAUD. Where's father, Uncle Ralph?

RALPH. With his solicitor.

ATHENE. We left Guy with mother at the studio. She still thinks she ought to come. She keeps on saying she must, now father's in a hole.

MAUD. I've got her things on the cab; she ought to be perfectly free to choose.

RALPH. You've got freedom on the brain, Maud.

MAUD. So would you, Uncle Ralph, if you had father about.

RALPH. I'm his partner, my dear.

MAUD. Yes; how do you manage him?

RALPH. I've never yet given him in charge.

ATHENE. What do you do, Uncle Ralph?

RALPH. Undermine him when I can.

MAUD. And when you can't?

RALPH. Undermine the other fellow. You can't go to those movie people now, Maud. They'd star you as the celebrated Maud Builder who gave her father into custody. Come to us instead, and have perfect freedom, till all this blows over.

MAUD. Oh! what will father be like now?

ATHENE. It's so queer you and he being brothers, Uncle Ralph.

RALPH. There are two sides to every coin, my dear. John's the head—and I'm the tail. He has the sterling qualities. Now, you girls have got to smooth him down, and make up to him. You've tried him pretty high.

MAUD. [Stubbornly] I never wanted him for a father, Uncle.

RALPH. They do wonderful things nowadays with inherited trouble. Come, are you going to be nice to him, both of you?

ATHENE. We're going to try.

RALPH. Good! I don't even now understand how it happened.

MAUD. When you went out with Guy, it wasn't three minutes before he came. Mother had just told us about—well, about something beastly. Father wanted us to go, and we agreed to go out for five minutes while he talked to mother. We went, and when we came back he told me to get a cab to take mother home. Poor mother stood there looking like a ghost, and he began hunting and hauling her towards the door. I saw red, and instead of a cab I fetched that policeman. Of course father did black his eye. Guy was splendid.

ATHENE. You gave him the lead.

MAUD. I couldn't help it, seeing father standing there all dumb.

ATHENE. It was awful! Uncle, why didn't you come back with Guy?

MAUD. Oh, yes! why didn't you, Uncle?

ATHENE. When Maud had gone for the cab, I warned him not to use force. I told him it was against the law, but he only said: "The law be damned!"

RALPH. Well, it all sounds pretty undignified.

MAUD. Yes; everybody saw red.

They have not seen the door opened from the hall, and BUILDER standing there. He is still unshaven, a little sunken in the face, with a glum, glowering expression. He has a document in his hand. He advances a step or two and they see him.

ATHENE and MAUD. [Aghast] Father!

BUILDER. Ralph, oblige me! See them off the premises!

RALPH. Steady, John!

BUILDER. Go!

MAUD. [Proudly] All right! We thought you might like to know that Athene's married, and that I've given up the movies. Now we'll go.

BUILDER turns his back on them, and, sitting down at his writing-table, writes. After a moment's whispered conversation with their Uncle, the two girls go out. RALPH BUILDER stands gazing with whimsical commiseration at his brother's back. As BUILDER finishes writing, he goes up and puts his hand on his brother's shoulder.

RALPH. This is an awful jar, old man!

BUILDER. Here's what I've said to that fellow: "MR MAYOR,—You had the effrontery to-day to discharge me with a caution—forsooth!—your fellow —magistrate. I've consulted my solicitor as to whether an action will lie for false imprisonment. I'm informed that it won't. I take this opportunity of saying that justice in this town is a travesty. I have no wish to be associated further with you or your fellows; but you are vastly mistaken if you imagine that I shall resign my position on the Bench or the Town Council.—Yours,

"JOHN BUILDER."

RALPH. I say—keep your sense of humour, old boy.

BUILDER. [Grimly] Humour? I've spent a night in a cell. See this! [He holds out the document] It disinherits my family.

RALPH. John!

BUILDER. I've done with those two ladies. As to my wife—if she doesn't come back—! When I suffer, I make others suffer.

RALPH. Julia's very upset, my dear fellow; we all are. The girls came here to try and—

BUILDER. [Rising] They may go to hell! If that lousy Mayor thinks I'm done with—he's mistaken! [He rings the bell] I don't want any soft sawder. I'm a fighter.

RALPH. [In a low voice] The enemy stands within the gate, old chap.

BUILDER. What's that?

RALPH. Let's boss our own natures before we boss those of other people. Have a sleep on it, John, before you do anything.

BUILDER. Sleep? I hadn't a wink last night. If you'd passed the night I had—

RALPH. I hadn't many myself.

TOPPING enters.

BUILDER. Take this note to the Mayor with my compliments, and don't bring back an answer.
TOPPING. Very good, sir. There's a gentleman from the "Comet" in the hall, sir. Would you see him for a minute, he says.

BUILDER. Tell him to go to—

A voice says, "Mr Builder!" BUILDER turns to see the figure of the JOURNALIST in the hall doorway. TOPPING goes out.

JOURNALIST. [Advancing with his card] Mr Builder, it's very good of you to see me. I had the pleasure this morning—I mean—I tried to reach you when you left the Mayor's. I thought you would probably have your own side of this unfortunate matter. We shall be glad to give it every prominence.

TOPPING has withdrawn, and RALPH BUILDER, at the window, stands listening.

BUILDER. [Drily, regarding the JOURNALIST, who has spoken in a pleasant and polite voice] Very good of you!

JOURNALIST. Not at all, sir. We felt that you would almost certainly have good reasons of your own which would put the matter in quite a different light.

BUILDER. Good reasons? I should think so! I tell you—a very little more of this liberty—licence I call it—and there isn't a man who'll be able to call himself head of a family.

JOURNALIST. [Encouragingly] Quite!

BUILDER. If the law thinks it can back up revolt, it's damned well mistaken. I struck my daughter—I was in a passion, as you would have been.

JOURNALIST. [Encouraging] I'm sure—

BUILDER. [Glaring at him] Well, I don't know that you would; you look a soft sort; but any man with any blood in him.

JOURNALIST. Can one ask what she was doing, sir? We couldn't get that point quite clear.

BUILDER. Doing? I just had my arm round my wife, trying to induce her to come home with me after a little family tiff, and this girl came at me. I lost my temper, and tapped her with my cane. And— that policeman brought by my own daughter—a policeman! If the law is going to enter private houses and abrogate domestic authority, where the hell shall we be?

JOURNALIST. [Encouraging] No, I'm sure—I'm sure!

BUILDER. The maudlin sentimentality in these days is absolutely rotting this country. A man can't be master in his own house, can't require his wife to fulfil her duties, can't attempt to control the conduct of his daughters, without coming up against it and incurring odium. A man can't control his employees; he can't put his foot down on rebellion anywhere, without a lot of humanitarians and licence-lovers howling at him.

JOURNALIST. Excellent, Sir; excellent!

BUILDER. Excellent? It's damnable. Here am I—a man who's always tried to do his duty in private life and public—brought up before the Bench— my God! because I was doing that duty; with a little too much zeal, perhaps—I'm not an angel!

JOURNALIST. No! No! of course.

BUILDER. A proper Englishman never is. But there are no proper Englishmen nowadays.

He crosses the room in his fervour.

RALPH. [Suddenly] As I look at faces—

BUILDER. [Absorbed] What! I told this young man I wasn't an angel.

JOURNALIST. [Drawing him on] Yes, Sir; I quite understand.

BUILDER. If the law thinks it can force me to be one of your weak-kneed sentimentalists who let everybody do what they like—

RALPH. There are a good many who stand on their rights left, John.

BUILDER. [Absorbed] What! How can men stand on their rights left?

JOURNALIST. I'm afraid you had a painful experience, sir.

BUILDER. Every kind of humiliation. I spent the night in a stinking cell. I haven't eaten since breakfast yesterday. Did they think I was going to eat the muck they shoved in? And all because in a moment of anger—which I regret, I regret!—I happened to strike my daughter, who was interfering between me and my wife. The thing would be funny if it weren't so disgusting. A man's house used to be sanctuary. What is it now? With all the world poking their noses in?

He stands before the fire with his head bent, excluding as it were his interviewer and all the world.

JOURNALIST. [Preparing to go] Thank you very much, Mr Builder. I'm sure I can do you justice. Would you like to see a proof?

BUILDER. [Half conscious of him] What?

JOURNALIST. Or will you trust me?

BUILDER. I wouldn't trust you a yard.

JOURNALIST. [At the door] Very well, sir; you shall have a proof, I promise. Good afternoon, and thank you.

BUILDER. Here!

But he is gone, and BUILDER is left staring at his brother, on whose face is still that look of whimsical commiseration.

RALPH. Take a pull, old man! Have a hot bath and go to bed.

BUILDER. They've chosen to drive me to extremes, now let them take the consequences. I don't care a kick what anybody thinks.

RALPH. [Sadly] Well, I won't worry you anymore, now.

BUILDER. [With a nasty laugh] No; come again to-morrow!

RALPH. When you've had a sleep. For the sake of the family name, John, don't be hasty.

BUILDER. Shut the stable door? No, my boy, the horse has gone.

RALPH. Well, Well!

With a lingering look at his brother, who has sat down sullenly at the writing table, he goes out into the hall. BUILDER remains staring in front of him. The dining-room door opens, and CAMILLE's head is thrust in. Seeing him, she draws back, but he catches sight of her.

BUILDER. Here!

CAMILLE comes doubtfully up to the writing table. Her forehead is puckered as if she were thinking hard.

BUILDER. [Looking at her, unsmiling] So you want to be my mistress, do you?

CAMILLE makes a nervous gesture.

Well, you shall. Come here.

CAMILLE. [Not moving] You f—frighten me.

BUILDER. I've paid a pretty price for you. But you'll make up for it; you and others.

CAMILLE. [Starting back] No; I don't like you to-day! No!

BUILDER. Come along! [She is just within reach and he seizes her arm] All my married life I've put a curb on myself for the sake of respectability. I've been a man of principle, my girl, as you saw yesterday. Well, they don't want that! [He draws her close] You can sit on my knee now.

CAMILLE. [Shrinking] No; I don't want to, to-day.

BUILDER. But you shall. They've asked for it!

CAMILLE. [With a supple movement slipping away from him] They? What is all that? I don't want any trouble. No, no; I am not taking any.

She moves back towards the door. BUILDER utters a sardonic laugh.

Oh! you are a dangerous man! No, no! Not for me! Good-bye, sare!

She turns swiftly and goes out. BUILDER again utters his glum laugh. And then, as he sits alone staring before him, perfect silence reigns in the room. Over the window-sill behind him a BOY'S face is seen to rise; it hangs there a moment with a grin spreading on it.

BOY'S VOICE. [Sotto] Johnny Builder!

As BUILDER turns sharply, it vanishes.

'Oo beat 'is wife?

BUILDER rushes to the window.

BOY'S VOICE. [More distant and a little tentative] Johnny Builder!

BUILDER. You little devil! If I catch you, I'll wring your blasted little neck!

BOY'S VOICE. [A little distant] 'Oo blacked the copper's eye?

BUILDER, in an ungovernable passion, seizes a small flower-pot from the sill and dings it with all his force. The sound of a crash.

BOY'S VOICE. [Very distant] Ya-a-ah! Missed!

BUILDER stands leaning out, face injected with blood, shaking his fist. The CURTAIN falls for a few seconds.


## SCENE III

Evening the same day.

BUILDER's study is dim and neglected-looking; the window is still open, though it has become night. A street lamp outside shines in, and the end of its rays fall on BUILDER asleep. He is sitting in a high chair at the fireside end of the writing-table, with his elbows on it, and his cheek resting on his hand. He is still unshaven, and his clothes unchanged. A Boy's head appears above the level of the window-sill, as if beheaded and fastened there.

BOY'S VOICE. [In a forceful whisper] Johnny Builder!

BUILDER stirs uneasily. The Boy's head vanishes. BUILDER, raising his other hand, makes a sweep before his face, as if to brush away a mosquito. He wakes. Takes in remembrance, and sits a moment staring gloomily before him. The door from the hall is opened and TOPPING comes in with a long envelope in his hand.

TOPPING. [Approaching] From the "Comet," sir. Proof of your interview, sir; will you please revise, the messenger says; he wants to take it back at once.

BUILDER. [Taking it] All right. I'll ring.

TOPPING. Shall I close in, sir?

BUILDER. Not now.

TOPPING withdraws. BUILDER turns up a standard lamp on the table, opens the envelope, and begins reading the galley slip. The signs of uneasiness and discomfort grow on him.

BUILDER. Did I say that? Muck! Muck! [He drops the proof, sits a moment moving his head and rubbing one hand uneasily on the surface of the table, then reaches out for the telephone receiver] Town, 245. [Pause] The "Comet"? John Builder. Give me the Editor. [Pause] That you, Mr Editor? John Builder speaking. That interview. I've got the proof. It won't do. Scrap the whole thing, please. I don't want to say anything. [Pause] Yes. I know I said it all; I can't help that. [Pause] No; I've changed my mind. Scrap it, please. [Pause] No, I will not say anything. [Pause] You can say what you dam' well please. [Pause] I mean it; if you put a word into my mouth, I'll sue you for defamation of character. It's undignified muck. I'm tearing it up. Good-night. [He replaces the receiver, and touches a bell; then, taking up the galley slip, he tears it viciously across into many pieces, and rams them into the envelope.]

TOPPING enters.

Here, give this to the messenger-sharp, and tell him to run with it.

TOPPING. [Whose hand can feel the condition of the contents, with a certain surprise] Yes, sir.

He goes, with a look back from the door.

The Mayor is here, sir. I don't know whether you would wish

BUILDER, rising, takes a turn up and down the room.

BUILDER. Nor do I. Yes! I'll see him.

TOPPING goes out, and BUILDER stands over by the fender, with his head a little down.

TOPPING. [Re-entering] The Mayor, sir.

He retires up Left. The MAYOR is overcoated, and carries, of all things, a top hat. He reaches the centre of the room before he speaks.

MAYOR. [Embarrassed] Well, Builder?

BUILDER. Well?

MAYOR. Come! That caution of mine was quite parliamentary. I 'ad to save face, you know.

BUILDER. And what about my face?

MAYOR. Well, you—you made it difficult for me. 'Ang it all! Put yourself into my place!

BUILDER. [Grimly] I'd rather put you into mine, as it was last night.

MAYOR. Yes, yes! I know; but the Bench has got a name to keep up—must stand well in the people's eyes. As it is, I sailed very near the wind. Suppose we had an ordinary person up before us for striking a woman?

BUILDER. I didn't strike a woman—I struck my daughter.

MAYOR. Well, but she's not a child, you know. And you did resist the police, if no worse. Come! You'd have been the first to maintain British justice. Shake 'ands!

BUILDER. Is that what you came for?

MAYOR. [Taken aback] Why—yes; nobody can be more sorry than I—

BUILDER. Eye-wash! You came to beg me to resign.

MAYOR. Well, it's precious awkward, Builder. We all feel—

BUILDER. Save your powder, Mayor. I've slept on it since I wrote you that note. Take my resignations.

MAYOR. [In relieved embarrassment] That's right. We must face your position.

BUILDER. [With a touch of grim humour] I never yet met a man who couldn't face another man's position.

MAYOR. After all, what is it?

BUILDER. Splendid isolation. No wife, no daughters, no Councillorship, no Magistracy, no future—[With a laugh] not even a French maid. And why? Because I tried to exercise a little wholesome family authority. That's the position you're facing, Mayor.

MAYOR. Dear, dear! You're devilish bitter, Builder. It's unfortunate, this publicity. But it'll all blow over; and you'll be back where you were. You've a good sound practical sense underneath your temper. [A pause] Come, now! [A pause] Well, I'll say good-night, then.

BUILDER. You shall have them in writing tomorrow.

MAYOR. [With sincerity] Come! Shake 'ands.

BUILDER, after a long look, holds out his hand. The two men exchange a grip.

The MAYOR, turning abruptly, goes out. BUILDER remains motionless for a minute, then resumes his seat at the side of the writing table, leaning his head on his hands. The Boy's head is again seen rising above the level of the window-sill, and another and another follows, till the three, as if decapitated, heads are seen in a row.

BOYS' VOICES. [One after another in a whispered crescendo] Johnny Builder! Johnny Builder! Johnny Builder!

BUILDER rises, turns and stares at them. The THREE HEADS disappear, and a Boy's voice cries shrilly: "Johnny Builder!" BUILDER moves towards the window; voices are now crying in various pitches and keys: "Johnny Builder!" "Beatey Builder!" "Beat 'is wife-er!" "Beatey Builder!" BUILDER stands quite motionless, staring, with the street lamp lighting up a queer, rather pitiful defiance on his face. The voices swell. There comes a sudden swish and splash of water, and broken yells of dismay.

TOPPING'S VOICE. Scat! you young devils!

The sound of scuffling feet and a long-drawnout and distant "Miaou!" BUILDER stirs, shuts the window, draws the curtains, goes to the armchair before the fireplace and sits down in it. TOPPING enters with a little tray on which is a steaming jug of fluid, some biscuits and a glass. He comes stealthily up level with the chair. BUILDER stirs and looks up at him.

TOPPING. Excuse me, sir, you must 'ave digested yesterday morning's breakfast by now—must live to eat, sir.

BUILDER. All right. Put it down.

TOPPING. [Putting the tray down on the table and taking up BUILDER'S pipe] I fair copped those young devils.

BUILDER. You're a good fellow.

TOPPING. [Filling the pipe] You'll excuse me, sir; the Missis—has come back, sir—

BUILDER stares at him and TOPPING stops. He hands BUILDER the filled pipe and a box of matches.

BUILDER. [With a shiver] Light the fire, Topping. I'm chilly.

While TOPPING lights the fire BUILDER puts the pipe in his mouth and applies a match to it. TOPPING, having lighted the fire, turns to go, gets as far as half way, then comes back level with the table and regards the silent brooding figure in the chair.

BUILDER. [Suddenly] Give me that paper on the table. No; the other one—the Will.

TOPPING takes up the Will and gives it to him.

TOPPING. [With much hesitation] Excuse me, sir. It's pluck that get's 'em 'ome, sir—begging your pardon.

BUILDER has resumed his attitude and does not answer.

[In a voice just touched with feeling] Good-night, sir.

BUILDER. [Without turning his head] Good-night.

TOPPING has gone. BUILDER sits drawing at his pipe between the firelight and the light from the standard lamp. He takes the pipe out of his mouth and a quiver passes over his face. With a half angry gesture he rubs the back of his hand across his eyes.

BUILDER. [To himself] Pluck! Pluck! [His lips quiver again. He presses them hard together, puts his pipe back into his mouth, and, taking the Will, thrusts it into the newly-lighted fire and holds it there with a poker.]

While he is doing this the door from the hall is opened quietly, and MRS BUILDER enters without his hearing her. She has a work bag in her hand. She moves slowly to the table, and stands looking at him. Then going up to the curtains she mechanically adjusts them, and still keeping her eyes on BUILDER, comes down to the table and pours out his usual glass of whisky toddy. BUILDER, who has become conscious of her presence, turns in his chair as she hands it to him. He sits a moment motionless, then takes it from her, and squeezes her hand. MRS BUILDER goes silently to her usual chair below the fire, and taking out some knitting begins to knit. BUILDER makes an effort to speak, does not succeed, and sits drawing at his pipe.

The CURTAIN falls.


## JOHN GALSWORHY – A SHORT BIOGRAPHY

John Galsworthy, eldest son of John Galsworthy (1817-1904), a solicitor and company director of Old Jewry, London, and Blanche Bailey (1835-1915), daughter of Charles Bartleet, a needlemaker in Redditch. His father's ancestors originated in Wembury, near Plymouth in England, and Galsworthy, for whom family origins were of significant importance, maintained a close connection with Devon. His more immediate family were considerably wealthy and well established in the shipping industry, and owned a fine estate in Kingston-upon-Thames called Parkfield, where Galsworthy was born on the 14th August 1867. At the age of nine he began education at Saugeen, a Bournemouth preparatory school, before starting at Harrow school in 1881 where he remained until 1886, distinguishing himself as an athlete.

His education at Harrow being successful enough to gain him entrance to Oxford, he began at New College to read law and gained a second-class degree with honours in 1889. Following Lincoln's Inn he was called to the bar in 1890. Despite this recognition he realised that he was not keen to actually begin practising law and so he resolved instead to look after the family's shipping business while specialising himself in Marine Law. This decision saw him take to the seas to destinations such as Vancouver, Island and South AFrica, though it was at the age of twenty-five on one particular journey to Australia, motivated by an (unfulfilled) intention to meet Robert Louis Stevenson on Samoa that he would being to realise fully his literary interests: though he was not considering becoming a writer at this time, his enjoyment of literature was enough to encourage an attempt at meeting a great writer and eventually enabled one of the most significant encounters of his life. He made the journey with his friend Edward Sanderson and, though he missed Stevenson, he met Joseph Conrad, a fellow future author famed for his novels which were often nautically themed. At the time Conrad was the first mate of the sailing-ship Torrens moored in the harbour of Adelaide, Australia; still very much focused on his ship-borne career, he was yet to begin his writing in earnest.

Indeed, though neither knew at the time, both Conrad and Galsworthy were at similar junctures in their lives, their time spent as sea acting as a transitional period during which each found their literary calling. It is perhaps owning to this unknown common ground that they became close friends. During his time on the Torrens Galsworthy recorded several details, offering a frank and valuable characterisation of Conrad while also illuminating his own experiences as a student of Marine Law.

"I supposed to be studying navigation for the Admiralty Bar, would every day work out the position of the ship with the captain. On one side of the saloon table we would sit and check our observations with those of Conrad, who from the other side of the table would look at us a little quizzically."

On his return to England and the cessation of his nautical voyaging, Galsworthy began an affair with the wife of his first cousin, Major Arthur John Galsworthy. Ada Nemesis Pearson Cooper (1864-1956), the daughter of Emanuel Copper, an obstetrician from Norwich, remained married to the Major for ten years and the affair remained secret for its duration. In order to conceal the affair they took considerable pains to avoid suspicion. One such tactic was to stay in a secluded farmhouse called Wingstone in the village on Manaton on Dartmoor, in Devon. In Galsworthy's decision to choose Devon as the location for their clandestine rendezvous we see evidence of Galsworthy's affection for the place of his father's origin. It was only when, in 1905, she divorced the Major that their affair became known following their marriage on 23rd September of that year.

Galsworthy now took to writing sometime after having met Conrad and his career began in earnest when, in 1897, his first work, From the Four Winds, a volume of short stories, was published under the pseudonym John Sinjohn. He succeeded this in 1898 with Jocelyn, his first novel, and then his second in 1900, Villa Rubein. In 1901 he published a second volume of short stories, A Man of Devon, which was the last of his work to be published under pseudonym. The first of his work to be published under his own name was The Island Pharisees in 1904, a novel of social observation, seasoned with flashes of satire and propaganda. His decision to write under his own name is arguably owing to the recent death of his father, either as a mark of respect to his name or because now he was able to publish freely without incurring the possibility of paternal disappointment at his choice of career. It also marked a shift in his professionalism; he had hitherto published with small, independent publishers, but The Island Pharisees was published by Heinemann, a far more established House and one with whom he remained for the duration of his writing career.

He arguably cemented his position and maturity as a writer when, in 1906, he saw the publication of both his first major play, The Silver Box, and the novel The Man of Property. Each was published to considerable critical acclaim, and to achieve both in such a short space of time was impressive. the Silver Box concerns the imbalance in the justice system with regards to criminals of differing class by contrasting the treatment of a poor thief and a rich thief, both of whom stole silver cigarette cases but for very different reasons. The complexity of individual experience when not dealt with in public is highlighted and questioned in a bravely critical manner; despite the clear issues it raises with class and privilege, the final night was attended by the Price and Princess of Wales. The Man of Property was the first novel in the famous The Forsyte Saga, a trilogy of novels with an 'interlude' between each one, written between 1906 and 1921. Dealing with the questions of status, class and materialism, The Man of Property introduces us to the Forsyte family, particularly Soames Forsyte, who is acutely aware of his status as 'new money' and equally keen to assert himself as a wealthy man. Jealous of his wife and desperate to own things in order to confirm his wealth to those observing him, he engineers a plan to keep his wife from her friends which backfires spectacularly when, instead of cutting her off, all Soames achieves is enabling her to have an affair. This drives Soames to terrible actions with terrible consequences, which Galsworthy depicts with confidence.

Very typically Edwardian, the novel focuses on conflict between property and art, and to a certain degree much of its emotional power is drawn from Galsworthy's own life, particularly his affair with Ada. Their rendezvous in the countryside of Devon mirror the manner in which Forsyte seeks to relocate his wife and; though theirs was a much healthier relationship, there are clear similarities. By examining the fragile nature of the class system and those moving within it Galsworthy offered an important perspective on the relationships between material wealth, personal happiness and obsession, and the manner in which these change over time. His contemporaries widely regarded the publication of this novel as marking the end of Victorianism. His friend Conrad praised it as "indubitably a piece of art" and, though the notoriously risqué D.H. Lawrence lamented the novel's timidity in the face of sexuality and sensuality, he considered it potentially "a very great novel, a very great satire".

Though he continued to write both plays and novels, it was his work as a playwright for which he was most celebrated by his contemporaries. Indeed, his next novel, The Country House, seems uncharacteristically unfocused, its satirical view of those belonging to the country set comparatively unremarkable and weakly characterised, while at times the tone of satire becomes one of ironic detachment. In 1909 he published Fraternity, an exploration of of the various connections between urban society and the social classes therein, though its representation of lower-class Londoners is utterly unconvincing and ill-informed. Remaining with the subject of the landed gentry and the society surrounding it, in 1915 he published The Freelands, which does not stray far from conservative discussions of capitalism, the rural economy and their interrelationship.

His drama, however, featured a convincingly muted realism, directed at a relatively small, educated and politically-aware audience. His social agenda is prevalent here too, and is represented in a simple and static manner producing arresting instances of high drama. This talent for creating moments of captivating theatre is complimented by an instinctual sense of balance enabling his narratives to vacillate between their emotional high- and low-points, ultimately reaching conclusive equilibrium. This is particularly evident in one of his most popular plays, Strife, published in 1909 and examining the antagonists in a strike at a Cornish tin mine. In this, and in 1910's Justice, he approaches his subject with sympathy, irony and balance, which establishes a position of narrative authority while garnering the audiences trust that he is representing his characters and their motives justly. Justice condemns the use of solitary confinement in prisons, a reformist agenda which caught the liberality of his contemporary audiences along with the home secretary, Winston Churchill. Despite he was careful to disassociate himself with politics and professed himself apolitical, he and his work were nevertheless aligned with the views of the Liberal establishment. He spent much of the duration of the First World War working in a field hospital in France as an orderly having been passed over for military service.

Despite the popularity and brilliance of his work, it was only in 1920 that he had his first true commercial success with The Skin Game, a melodrama dealing with ethics, property and class. The play was adapted by Alfred Hitchcock in 1931. Galsworthy, meanwhile, had turned down a knighthood in 1918, considering his work not sufficient to be made a knight of the realm. He did, however, accept the Belgian Palmes d'Or in the following year. In 1920 he published the second novel in the Forsyte Saga, In Chancery, in which he resumes many of the themes of the first novel, focusing on the marital disharmony between Soames Forsyte and his wife. Katherine Mansfield considered it "a fascinating, brilliant book" in her review in The Atheneum. Then, in 1921, he was elected as the PEN International Literary Club's first president. The concluding novel to The Forsyte

Saga, To Let was published in 1921 with a kind of peace being found between Forsyte and his now-ex wife, though he is left contemplating his losses and his greed. More ironic treatment of class confusions followed in Loyalties, bringing with it more popular success which lasted until 1926 and Escape, the last of his popular plays. Though he enjoyed popular success it was inconsistent and relatively small. His Collected Plays was published in 1929.

Over the course of time the appreciation of his work has gradually shifted from his plays to his novels, and particularly the detail and intricacy of his chronicle of English social difference, tension and pretension in The Forsyte Saga. Its success encouraged Galsworthy to revisit Soames Forsyte in a second trilogy, A Modern Comedy, which follows Soames's obsessive love of his daughter Fleur. In its three volumes, The White Monkey (1924), The Silver Spoon (1936) and Swan Song (1928) he examines the English commercial upper-middle class and its ideologies, its instinct to possess as its only way of distinguishing itself manifested in the poisonous materialism of Soames. Interestingly, this emergent social class which he so vehemently criticises is the very class from which he emerged. He witnessed first-hand its insularity, its chauvinism, its restrictive and oppressive morality, its stubborn imperialism and its materialism, and it is this experience which enables him to write so comfortably about it. Swan Song is widely considered among the best of Galsworthy's writing for the depth of its exploration of society and its heightened emotional subtlety. In 1929 he was appointed to the Order of Merit, despite having turned down a knighthood earlier. He spent his last years writing a third trilogy, End of the Chapter, beginning in 1931 with Maid in Waiting, Flowering Wilderness in 1932 and concluding with Over The River in 1933. These are significantly less coherent works and are indicative of his deteriorating health. Indeed, in 1932 he was awarded the Nobel Prize, though he was too ill to attend the ceremony.

Throughout the course of his career he received honorary degrees from the universities of St Andrews (1922), Manchester (1927), Dublin (1929), Cambridge (1930), Sheffield (1930), Oxford (1931), and Princeton (1931). In 1926 New College, Oxford, elected him as an honorary fellow. In photographs he is portrayed as handsome, fastidiously dressed and dignified. He was unusually compassionate and this saw him involved in several charitable and humane causes throughout the course of his life, including penal reforms, attacks on theatrical censorship and campaigning for animal rights. Though he spent the majority of the final seven years of his life at his home in Bury, West Sussex, it was at his home in Hampstead, London, that he died of a brain tumour on 31st January, 1933, six weeks after having been too ill to attend the ceremony in honour of his receiving the Nobel Prize. According to demands made in his will he was cremated and his ashes scattered over the South Downs from an aeroplane. Also in his will was his wish to leave cottages to several of his astonished tenants. He is memorialised in Highgate 'New' Cemetery and in the cloisters of New College, Oxford, where he was an honorary fellow.

www.ingramcontent.com/pod-product-compliance
Lightning Source LLC
Chambersburg PA
CBHW061455170626
46811CB00004B/1524